Dear Reader,

Looking back over the years, I find it hard to realise that thirty of them have gone by since I wrote my first book—*Sister Peters in Amsterdam*. It wasn't until I started writing about her that I found that once I had started writing, nothing was going to make me stop—and at that time I had no intention of sending it to a publisher. It was my daughter who urged me to try my luck.

I shall never forget the thrill of having my first book accepted. A thrill I still get each time a new story is accepted. Writing to me is such a pleasure, and seeing a story unfolding on my old typewriter is like watching a film and wondering how it will end. Happily of course.

To have so many of my books re-published is such a delightful thing to happen and I can only hope that those who read them will share my pleasure in seeing them on the bookshelves again...and enjoy reading them

## Back by Popular Demand

A collector's edition of favourite titles from one of the world's best-loved romance authors. Mills & Boon® are proud to bring back these sought after titles and present them as one cherished collection.

## *BETTY NEELS: COLLECTOR'S EDITION*

# A CHRISTMAS PROPOSAL

## BY
## BETTY NEELS

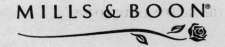

MILLS & BOON®

A Christmas Proposal *was first published in Great Britain 1996 by*
Mills & Boon Limited *and* A Christmas Romance *was first published
in Great Britain 1999 by Mills & Boon Limited*
*This edition 2001*
*Harlequin Mills & Boon Limited,*
*Eton House, 18-24 Paradise Road, Richmond, Surrey TW9 1SR*

A CHRISTMAS PROPOSAL © Betty Neels 1996
A CHRISTMAS ROMANCE © Betty Neels 1999

ISBN 0 263 82838 7

73-1201

*Printed and bound in Spain
by Litografia Rosés S.A., Barcelona*

# CHAPTER ONE

THE girl standing in a corner of the crowded room hardly merited a second glance; she was small, with light brown hair strained back into an unfashionable bun, a face whose snub nose and wide mouth did nothing to redeem its insignificance, and she was wearing an elaborate shrimp-pink dress. But after his first glance the man standing across the room from her looked again. Presently he strolled over to stand beside her. His 'Hello' was pleasant and she turned her head to look at him.

She answered him politely, studying him from large brown eyes fringed by curling lashes. Looking at her eyes, he reflected that one soon forgot the nose and mouth and dragged-back hair. He smiled down at her. 'Do you know anyone here? I came with friends—I'm staying with them and was asked to come along with them. A birthday party, isn't it?'

'Yes.' She looked past him to the crowded room, the groups of laughing, gossiping people waving to each other with drinks in their hands, the few couples dancing in the centre. 'Would you like me to introduce you to someone?'

He said in his friendly way, 'You know everyone here? Is it your birthday?'

'Yes.' She gave him a quick surprised look and bent her head to examine the beaded bodice of her dress.

'Then shouldn't you be the belle of the ball?'

'Oh, it's not my party. It's my stepsister's—that pretty girl over by the buffet. Would you like to meet Clare?'

'The competition appears too keen at the moment,' he said easily. 'Shouldn't you be sharing the party, since it's your birthday too?'

'Well, no.' She had a pretty voice and she spoke matter-of-factly. 'I'm sure you'd like to meet some of the guests. I don't know your name...'

'Forgive me. Hay-Smythe—Oliver.'

'Bertha Soames.' She put out a small hand and he shook it gently.

'I really don't want to meet anyone. I think that perhaps I'm a little on the old side for them.'

She scrutinised him gravely—a very tall, strongly built man, with fair hair thickly sprinkled with grey. His eyes were grey too, and he had the kind of good looks which matched his assured air.

'I don't think you're in the least elderly,' she told him.

He thanked her gravely and added, 'Do you not dance?'

'Oh, I love to dance.' She smiled widely at him,

but as quickly the smile faded. 'I—that is, my step-mother asked me to see that everyone was enjoying themselves. That's why I'm standing here—if I see anyone on their own I make sure that they've got a drink and meet someone. I really think that you should...'

'Definitely not, Miss Soames.' He glanced down at her and thought how out of place she looked in the noisy room. And why, if it was her birthday, was she not wearing a pretty dress and not that ill-fitting, over-elaborate garment? 'Are you hungry?'

'Me? Hungry?' She nodded her head. 'Yes, I missed lunch.' Her eyes strayed to the buffet, where a number of people were helping themselves lavishly to the dainties upon it. 'Why don't you...?'

Dr Hay-Smythe, hard-working in his profession and already respected by older colleagues, a man who would never pass a stray kitten or a lost dog and who went out of his way to make life easy for anyone in trouble, said now, 'I'm hungry too. Supposing we were to slip away and have a meal somewhere? I don't imagine we should be missed, and we could be back long before this finishes.'

She stared at him. 'You mean go somewhere outside? But there isn't a café anywhere near here—besides...'

'Even Belgravia must have its pubs. Anyway, I've my car outside—we can look around.'

Her eyes shone. 'I'd like that. Must I tell my stepmother?'

'Certainly not. This door behind you—where does it lead? A passage to the hall? Let us go now.'

'I'll have to get my coat,' said Bertha when they were in the hall. 'I won't be long, but it's at the top of the house.'

'Haven't you a mac somewhere down here?'

'Yes, but it's very old…'

His smile reassured her. 'No one will notice in the pub.' He reflected that at least it would conceal that dreadful dress.

So, suitably shrouded, she went out of the house with him, through the important front door, down the imposing steps and onto the pavement.

'Just along here,' said the doctor, gesturing to where a dark grey Rolls-Royce was parked. He unlocked the door, popped her inside and got in beside her. As he drove off he asked casually, 'You live here with your parents?'

'Yes. Father is a lawyer—he does a lot of work for international companies. My stepmother prefers to live here in London.'

'You have a job?'

'No.' She turned her head to look out of the window, and he didn't pursue the subject but talked idly about this and that as he left the quiet streets with their stately houses and presently, in a narrow street bustling with people, stopped the car by an empty meter. 'Shall we try that pub on the corner?' he suggested, and helped her out.

Heads turned as they went in; they made an odd couple—he in black tie and she in a shabby raincoat—but the landlord waved them to a table in one corner of the saloon bar and then came over to speak to the doctor.

'Ain't seen yer for a while, Doc. Everything OK?'

'Splendid, thank you, Joe. How is your wife?'

'Fighting fit, thanks to you. What'll it be?' He glanced at Bertha. 'And the little lady here? A nice drop of wine for her?'

'We're hungry, Joe...'

'The wife's just this minute dished up bangers and mash. How about that, with a drop of old and mild?'

Dr Hay-Smythe raised an eyebrow at Bertha, and when she nodded Joe hurried away, to return presently with the beer and the wine and, five minutes later, a laden tray.

The homely fare was well cooked, hot and generous. The pair of them ate and drank in a friendly silence until the doctor said quietly, 'Will you tell me something about yourself?'

'There's nothing to tell. Besides, we're strangers; we're not likely to meet again.' She added soberly, 'I think I must be a little mad to be doing this.'

'Well, now, I can't agree with that. Madness, if at all, lies with people who go to parties and eat too much and drink too much and don't enjoy themselves. Whereas you and I have eaten food we enjoy and are content with each other's company.' He waited while Joe brought the coffee he had ordered. 'Being strangers, we can safely talk knowing that whatever we say will certainly be forgotten.'

'I've never met anyone like you before,' said Bertha.

'I'm perfectly normal; there must be thousands exactly like me.' He smiled a little. 'I think that perhaps you haven't met many people. Do you go out much? The theatre? Concerts? Sports club? Dancing?'

Bertha shook her head. 'Well, no. I do go shopping, and I take my stepmother's dog out and help when people come for tea or dinner. That kind of thing.'

'And your sister?' He saw her quick look. 'Stepsister Clare—has she a job?'

'No—she's very popular, you see, and she goes out a great deal and has lots of friends. She's pretty—you must have seen that...'

'Very pretty,' he agreed gravely. 'Why are you unhappy, Bertha? You don't mind my calling you Bertha? After all, as you said, we are most unlikely to meet again. I'm a very good listener. Think of me as an elder brother or, if you prefer, someone who is going to the other side of the world and never returning.'

She asked, 'How do you know that I'm unhappy?'

'If I tell you that I'm a doctor, does that answer your question?'

She smiled her relief. 'A doctor! Oh, then I could talk to you, couldn't I?'

His smile reassured her.

'You see, Father married again—oh, a long time ago, when I was seven years old. My mother died when I was five, and I suppose he was lonely, so he married my stepmother.

'Clare was two years younger than I. She was a lovely little girl and everyone adored her. I did too. But my stepmother—you see, I've always been plain and dull. I'm sure she tried her best to love me, and it must be my fault, because I tried to love her, but somehow I couldn't.

'She always treated me the same as Clare—we both had pretty dresses and we had a nice nanny and went to the same school—but even Father could see that I wasn't growing up to be a pretty girl like Clare, and my stepmother persuaded him that it would be better for me to stay at home and learn to be a good housewife...'

'Was Clare not a partner in this, too?'

'Well, no. She has always had lots of friends—

I mean, she hadn't time to be at home very much. She's really kind to me.' She laid a hand on a glimpse of pink frill which had escaped from the raincoat. 'She gave me this dress.'

'You have no money of your own?'

'No. Mother left me some, but I—I don't need it, do I?'

The doctor didn't comment on that. All he said was, 'There is a simple solution. You must find a job.'

'I'd like that, but I'm not trained for anything.' She added anxiously, 'I shouldn't have said all that to you. Please forget it. I have no right to complain.'

'Hardly complaining. Do you not feel better for talking about it?'

'Yes, oh, yes. I do.' She caught sight of the clock and gave a little gasp. 'Heavens, we've been here for ages...'

'Plenty of time,' said the doctor easily. 'I dare say the party will go on until midnight.' He paid the bill and stowed her in the Rolls once more, then drove her back and went with her into the house. Bertha shed the raincoat in the hall, smoothed the awful dress and went with him into the vast drawing room. The first person to see them was her stepmother.

'Bertha, where have you been? Go at once to the kitchen and tell Cook to send up some more

vol-au-vents. You're here to make yourself useful—'

Mrs Soames, suddenly aware of the doctor
standing close by, became all at once a different
woman. 'Run along, dear.' She spoke in a quite
different voice now, and added, 'Don't be long—
I'm sure your friends must be missing you.'

Bertha said nothing, and slipped away without a
glance at the doctor.

'Such a dear girl,' enthused Mrs Soames, her
massive front heaving with pseudo maternal feelings, 'and such a companion and help to me. It is
a pity that she is so shy and awkward. I have done
my best—' she managed to sound plaintive '—but
Bertha is an intelligent girl and knows that she is
lacking in looks and charm. I can only hope that
some good man will come along and marry her.'

She lifted a wistful face to her companion, who
murmured the encouraging murmur at which doctors are so good. 'But I mustn't bother you with
my little worries, must I? Come and talk to Clare—
she loves a new face. Do you live in London? We
must see more of you.'

So when Bertha returned he was at the other end
of the room, and Clare was laughing up at him, a
hand on his arm. Well, what did I expect? reflected
Bertha, and went in search of Crook the butler, a
lifelong friend and ally; she had had a good supper,
and now, fired by a rebellious spirit induced by Dr

Hay-Smythe's company, she was going to have a glass of champagne.

She tossed it off under Crook's fatherly eye, then took a second glass from his tray and drank that too. Probably she would have a headache later, and certainly she would have a red nose, but since there was no one to mind she really didn't care. She wished suddenly that her father were at home. He so seldom was…

People began to leave, exchanging invitations and greetings, several of them saying a casual goodbye to Bertha, who was busy finding coats and wraps and mislaid handbags. Dr Hay-Smythe was amongst the first to leave with his party, and he came across the hall to wish her goodbye.

'That was a splendid supper,' he observed, smiling down at her. 'Perhaps we might do it again some time.'

Before she could answer, Clare had joined them. 'Darling Oliver, don't you dare run off just as I've discovered how nice you are. I shall find your number in the phone book and ring you—you may take me out to dinner.'

'I'm going away for some weeks,' he said blandly. 'Perhaps it would be better if I phoned you when I get back.'

Clare pouted. 'You wretched man. All right, if that's the best you can do.'

She turned her head to look at Bertha. 'Mother's looking for you...'

Bertha went, but not before putting out a small, capable hand and having it shaken gently. Her, 'Goodbye Doctor,' was uttered very quietly.

It was after Bertha had gone to her bed in the modest room on the top floor of the house that Mrs Soames went along to her daughter's bedroom.

'A successful evening, darling,' she began. 'What do you think of that new man—Oliver Hay-Smythe? I was talking to Lady Everett about him. It seems he's quite well-known—has an excellent practice in Harley Street. Good family and plenty of money—old money...' She patted Clare's shoulder. 'Just the thing for my little girl.'

'He's going away for a while,' said Clare. 'He said he'd give me a ring when he gets back.' She looked at her mother and smiled. Then she frowned. 'How on earth did Bertha get to know him? They seemed quite friendly. Probably he's sorry for her—she did look a dowd, didn't she?'

Clare nibbled at a manicured hand. 'She looked happy—as though they were sharing a secret or something. Did you know that he has a great deal to do with backward children? He wouldn't be an easy man... If he shows an interest in Bertha, I shall encourage him.' She met her mother's eyes in the mirror. 'I may be wrong, but I don't think he's much of a party man—the Paynes, who brought him, told me that he's not married and there are no girlfriends—too keen on his work. If he wants to see more of Bertha, I'll be all sympathy!'

The two of them smiled at each other.

Dr Hay-Smythe parted from his friends at their house and took himself off to his flat over his consulting rooms. Cully, his man, had gone to his bed, but there was coffee warm on the Aga in the kitchen and a covered plate of sandwiches. He poured himself a mug of coffee and sat down at the kitchen table, and the Labrador who had been snoozing by the Aga got up sleepily and came to sit beside him, ready to share his sandwiches. He shared his master's thoughts too, chewing on cold roast beef and watching his face.

'I met a girl this evening, Freddie—a plain girl with beautiful eyes and wearing a truly awful frock. An uninteresting creature at first glance, but somehow I feel that isn't a true picture. She has a delightful voice—very quiet. She needs to get away from that ghastly stepmother too. I must think of something…'

Bertha, happily unaware of these plans for her future, slept all night, happier in her dreams than in her waking hours.

\*     \*     \*

It was two days later that the doctor saw a way to help Bertha. Not only did he have a private practice, a consultancy at two of the major hospitals and a growing reputation in his profession, he was also a partner in a clinic in the East End of London, dealing with geriatrics and anyone else who could not or would not go to Outpatients at any of the hospitals.

He had spent the evening there and his last patient had been an old lady, fiercely independent and living on her own in a tiny flat near the clinic. There wasn't a great deal he could do for her; a hard working life and old age were taking their toll, but she stumped around with a stick, refusing to go into an old people's home, declaring that she could look after herself.

'I'm as good as you, Doctor,' she declared after he had examined her. 'But I miss me books—can't read like I used to and I likes a good book. The social lady brought me a talking book, but it ain't the same as a real voice, if yer sees what I mean.' She added, 'A nice, quiet voice…'

He remembered Bertha then. 'Mrs Duke, would you like someone to come and read to you? Twice or three times a week, for an hour or so?'

'Not if it's one of them la-de-da ladies. I likes a nice bit of romance, not prosy stuff out of the parish mag.'

'The young lady I have in mind isn't at all like

that. I'm sure she will read anything you like. Would you like to give it a try? If it doesn't work out, we'll think of something else.'

'OK, I'll 'ave a go. When'll she come?'

'I shall be here again in two days' time in the afternoon. I'll bring her and leave her with you while I am here and collect her when I've finished. Would that suit you?'

'Sounds all right.' Mrs Duke heaved herself out of her chair and he got up to open the door for her. 'Be seeing yer.'

The doctor went home and laid his plans; Mrs Soames wasn't going to be easy, a little strategy would be needed…

Presently he went in search of Cully. Cully had been with him for some years, was middle-aged, devoted and a splendid cook. He put down the silver he was polishing and listened to the doctor.

'You would like me to telephone now, sir?'

'Please.'

'And if the lady finds the time you wish to visit her unacceptable?'

'She won't, Cully.'

Cully went to the phone on the wall and the doctor wandered to the old-fashioned dresser and chose an apple. Presently Cully put back the receiver.

'Five o'clock tomorrow afternoon, sir. Mrs Soames will be delighted.'

The doctor took a bite. 'Splendid, Cully. If at any time she should ring me here, or her daughter, be circumspect, if you please.'

Cully allowed himself to smile. 'Very good, sir.'

The doctor was too busy during the next day to give much thought to his forthcoming visit; he would have liked more time to think up reasons for his request, but he presented himself at five o'clock at Mrs Soames' house and was shown into the drawing room by a grumpy maid.

Mrs Soames, encased in a vivid blue dress a little too tight for her ample curves, rose to meet him. 'Oliver, how delightful to see you—I'm sure you must be a very busy man. I hear you have a large practice.' She gave rather a shrill laugh. 'A pity that I enjoy such splendid health or I might visit your rooms.'

He murmured appropriately and she patted the sofa beside her. 'Now, do tell me why you wanted to see me—' She broke off as Clare came into the room. Her surprise was very nearly real. 'Darling, you're back. See who has come to see us.'

Clare gave him a ravishing smile. 'And about time, too. I thought you were going away.'

'So did I.' He had stood up when she'd joined them, and he now took a chair away from the sofa. 'A series of lectures, but they have been postponed for a couple of weeks.'

Clare wrinkled her nose enchantingly. 'Good; now you can take me out to dinner.'

'A pleasure. I'll look in my appointments book and give you a ring, if I may. I was wondering if you have any time to spare during your days? I'm looking for someone who would be willing to read aloud for an hour or two several times a week to an old lady.' He smiled at Clare. 'You, Clare?'

'Me? Read a boring book to a boring old woman? Besides, I never have a moment to myself. What kind of books?'

'Oh, romances...'

'Yuk. How absolutely grim. And you thought of me, Oliver?' She gave a tinkling laugh. 'I don't even read to myself—only *Vogue* and *Tatler*.'

The doctor looked suitably disappointed. 'Ah, well, I dare say I shall be able to find someone else.'

Clare hesitated. 'Who is this old woman? Someone I know? I believe Lady Power has to have something done to her eyes, and there's Mrs Dillis—you know, she was here the other evening—dripping with diamonds and quite able to afford half a dozen companions or minders or whatever they're called.'

'Mrs Duke lives in a tiny flat on her own and she exists on her pension.'

'How ghastly.' Clare looked up and caught her mother's eye. 'Why shouldn't Bertha make herself useful? She's always reading anyway, and she never does anything or goes anywhere. Of course—that's the very thing.'

Clare got up and rang the bell, and when the grumpy maid came she told her to fetch Miss Bertha.

Bertha came into the room quietly and stopped short when she saw Dr Hay-Smythe.

'Come here, Bertha,' said Mrs Soames. 'You know Dr Hay-Smythe, I dare say? He was at Clare's party. He has a request to make and I'm sure you will agree to it—something to keep you occupied from time to time. Perhaps you will explain, Oliver.'

He had stood up when Bertha had come into the room, and when she sat down he came to sit near her. 'Yes, we have met,' he said pleasantly. 'I came to ask Clare to read to an old lady—a patient of mine—whose eyesight is failing, but she suggested that you might like to visit her. I believe you enjoy reading?'

'Yes, yes, I do.'

'That's settled, then,' said Mrs Soames. 'She's at your disposal, Oliver.'

'Would you like to go to this lady's flat—say, three times a week in the afternoons—and read to her for an hour or so?'

'Yes, thank you, Doctor.' Bertha sounded politely willing, but her eyes, when she looked at him, shone.

'Splendid. Let me see. Could you find your way to my rooms in Harley Street tomorrow afternoon? Then my secretary will give you her address. It is quite a long bus ride, but it won't be too busy in the afternoon. Come about two o'clock, will you? And thank you so much.'

'You'll have a drink, won't you?' asked Mrs Soames. 'I must make a phone call, but Clare will look after you. Bertha, will you go and see Cook and get her list for shopping tomorrow?'

The doctor, having achieved his purpose, sat for another half-hour, drinking tonic water while Clare drank vodka.

'Don't you drink?' She laughed at him. 'Really, Oliver, I should have thought you a whisky man.'

He smiled his charming smile. 'I'm driving. It would never do to reel into hospital, would it?'

'I suppose not. But why work in a hospital when you've got a big practice and can pick and choose?'

He said lightly, 'I enjoy the work.' He glanced at his watch. 'I am most reluctant to go, but I have an appointment. Thank you for the drink. I'll take you out to dinner and give you champagne at the first opportunity.'

She walked with him to the door, laid a pretty little hand on his arm and looked up at him. 'You don't mind? That I don't want to go to that old woman? I can't bear poverty and old, dirty people and smelly children. I think I must be very sensitive.'

He smiled a little. 'Yes, I am sure you are, and I don't mind in the least. I am sure your stepsister will manage very well—after all, all I asked for was someone to read aloud, and she seems to have time on her hands.'

'I'm really very sorry for her—her life is so dull,' declared Clare, and contrived to look as though she meant that.

Dr Hay-Smythe patted her hand, removed it from his sleeve, shook it and said goodbye with beautiful manners, leaving Clare to dance away and find her mother and gloat over her conquest.

As for the doctor, he went home well pleased with himself. He found Clare not at all to his taste but he had achieved his purpose.

It was raining as Bertha left the house the following afternoon to catch a bus, which meant that she had to wear the shabby mackintosh again. She consoled herself with the thought that it concealed the dress she was wearing—one which Clare had bought on the spur of the moment and disliked as soon as she'd got home with it.

It was unsuitable for a late autumn day, and a wet one, being of a thin linen—the colour of which was quite brilliant. But until her stepmother decided that Bertha might have something more seasonal there was nothing much else in her wardrobe suitable for the occasion, and anyway, nobody would see her. The old lady she was to visit had poor eyesight...

She got off the bus and walked the short distance to Dr Hay-Smythe's rooms, rang the bell and was admitted. His rooms were elegant and restful, and the cosy-looking lady behind the desk in the waiting room had a pleasant smile. 'Miss Soames?' She had got up and was opening a door beside the desk. 'The doctor's expecting you.'

Bertha hadn't been expecting him! She hung back to say, 'There's no need to disturb him. I was only to get the address from you.'

The receptionist merely smiled and held the door wide open, allowing Bertha to glimpse the doctor at his desk. He looked up then, stood up and came to meet her at the door.

'Hello, Bertha. Would you mind waiting until I finish this? A few minutes only. Take this chair. You found your way easily?' He pushed forward a small, comfortable chair, sat her down and went back to his own chair. 'Do undo your raincoat; it's warm in here.'

He was friendly and easy and she lost her shyness and settled comfortably, undoing her raincoat to reveal the dress. The doctor blinked at its startling colour as he picked up his pen. Another of Clare's cast-offs, he supposed, which cruelly high-lighted Bertha's nondescript features. Really, he reflected angrily, something should be done, but surely that was for her father to do? He finished his writing and left his chair.

'I'm going to the clinic to see one or two patients. I'll take you to Mrs Duke and pick you up when I've finished. Will you wait for me there?' He noticed the small parcel she was holding. 'Books? How thoughtful of you.'

'Well, Cook likes romances and she let me have some old paperbacks. They may please Mrs Duke.'

They went out together and the receptionist got up from her desk.

'Mrs Taylor, I'm taking Miss Soames with me. If I'm not back by five o'clock, lock up, will you? I've two appointments for this evening, haven't I? Leave the notes on my desk, will you?'

'Yes, Doctor. Sally will be here at six o'clock...'

'Sally is my nurse,' observed the doctor. 'My right hand. Mrs Taylor is my left hand.'

'Go on with you, Doctor,' said Mrs Taylor, and chuckled in a motherly way.

Bertha, brought up to make conversation when the occasion warranted it, worked her way pains-takingly through a number of suitable subjects in the Rolls-Royce, and the doctor, secretly amused, replied in his kindly way, so that by the time he drew up in a shabby street lined with small terraced houses she felt quite at ease.

He got out, opened her door and led the way across the narrow pavement to knock on a door woefully in need of a paintbrush. It was opened after a few moments by an old lady with a wrinkled face, fierce black eyes and an untidy head of hair. She nodded at the doctor and peered at Bertha.

'Brought that girl, 'ave yer? Come on in, then. I could do with a bit of company.' She led the way down the narrow hall to a door at the end. 'I've got me own flat,' she told Bertha. 'What's yer name?'

'Bertha, Mrs Duke.'

The doctor, watching her, saw with relief that she had neither wrinkled her small nose at the strong smell of cabbage and cats, nor had she let her face register anything other than friendly interest.

He didn't stay for more than a few minutes, and when he had gone Bertha, bidden to sit herself down, did so and offered the books she had brought.

Mrs Duke peered at their titles. 'Just me cup of tea,' she pronounced. 'I'll 'ave *Love's Undying Purpose* for a start.' She settled back in a sagging armchair and an elderly cat climbed onto her lap.

Bertha turned to the first page and began to read.

## CHAPTER TWO

BERTHA was still reading when the doctor returned
two hours later. There had been a brief pause while
Mrs Duke had made tea, richly brown and laced
with tinned milk and a great deal of sugar, but
Bertha hadn't been allowed to linger over it. She
had obediently picked up the book again and, with
a smaller cat on her own knees, had continued the
colourful saga of misunderstood heroine and
swashbuckling hero.

Mrs Duke had listened avidly to every word,
occasionally ordering her to 'read that bit again',
and now she got up reluctantly to let the doctor in.

'Enjoyed yourselves?' he wanted to know.

'Not 'arf. Reads a treat, she does. 'Artway
through the book already.' Mrs Duke subsided into
her chair again, puffing a bit. 'Bertha's a bit of all
right. When's she coming again?'

He looked at Bertha, sitting quietly with the cat
still on her knee.

'When would you like to come again?' he asked
her.

'Whenever Mrs Duke would like me to.'

'Tomorrow? We could finish this story…'

'Yes, of course. If I come about the same time?'

'Suits me. 'Ere, give me Perkins—like cats, do you?'

'Yes, they're good company, aren't they?' Bertha got up. 'We'll finish the story tomorrow,' she promised.

In the car the doctor said, 'I'll bring you over at the same time and collect you later. I want to take a look at Mrs Duke; she's puffing a bit.'

'Yes—she would make tea and she got quite breathless. Is she ill?'

'Her heart's worn out and so are her lungs. She's turned eighty and had a very hard life. She refuses to go into hospital. You have made her happy reading to her—thank you, Bertha.' She smiled and he glanced at her. 'You didn't find the smells and the cats too much for you?'

'No, of course not. Would she be offended if I took a cake or biscuits? I'm sure Cook will let me have something.'

'Would you? I think she would be delighted; she's proud, but she's taken to you, hasn't she?'

He reflected with some surprise that he had rather taken to Bertha himself...

'Could we settle on which days you would like to visit Mrs Duke? I'll bring you tomorrow, as I've already said, but supposing we say three times a week? Would Monday, Wednesday and Friday suit you? Better still, not Friday but Saturday—I dare say that will help her over the weekend. I'll give you a lift on Wednesdays and Saturdays and on Mondays, if you will come to my rooms as usual, there will be someone to take you to Mrs Duke.'

'I'll go any day you wish me to, but I must ask my stepmother… And I can get a bus—there's no need…'

'I go anyway. You might just as well have a lift. And on Mondays there is always someone going to the clinic—I'm one of several who work there.'

'Well, that would be nice, if you are sure it's no trouble?'

'None whatsoever. Is your stepmother likely to object to your going?'

'I don't think so.' Bertha paused. 'But she might not like me going with you…' She spoke matter-of-factly.

'Yes. Perhaps you are right. There is no need to mention that, is there?'

'You mean it will be a kind of secret between us?'

'Why not?' He spoke lightly and added, 'I'm taking your stepsister out to dinner tomorrow evening. She is a very popular girl, isn't she?'

Which somehow spoilt Bertha's day.

Two weeks went by and autumn showed signs of turning into winter. Mrs Soames had decided that Bertha, since she went out so seldom, needed no new dresses; Clare had several from last year still in perfect condition. A little alteration here and there and they would be quite all right for Bertha, she declared, making a mental note that she would have to buy something new for the girl when her father returned in a month's time.

So Bertha, decked out more often than not in a hastily altered outfit of Clare's—lime-green and too wide on the shoulders—went on her thrice-weekly visits to Mrs Duke: the highlights of her week. She liked Wednesdays and Saturdays best, of course, because then she was taken there by the doctor, but the young man who drove her there on Mondays was nice too. He was a doctor, recently qualified, who helped out at the clinic from time to time. They got on well together, for Bertha was a good listener, and he always had a great deal to say about the girl he hoped to marry.

It had surprised Bertha that her stepmother hadn't objected to her reading sessions with Mrs Duke, but that lady, intent on finding a suitable husband for Clare, would have done a good deal to nurture a closer friendship with Dr Hay-Smythe. That he had taken Clare out to dinner and accepted an invitation to dine with herself, Clare and a few friends she took as a good sign.

Clare had looked her best at the dinner party, in a deceptively simple white dress. Bertha had been there, of course, for there had been no good reason for her not to be, wearing the frightful pink frock again—quite unsuitable, but really, when the girl went out so seldom there was no point in buying her a lot of clothes.

Dr Hay-Smythe had been a delightful guest, Mrs Soames had noted, paying court to her darling Clare and treating Bertha with a friendly courtesy but at the same time showing no interest in the girl. Very satisfactory, Mrs Soames had reflected, heaving such a deep sigh that her corsets creaked.

It was at the end of the third week on the Saturday that Mrs Duke died. Bertha had just finished the third chapter of a novel that the old lady had particularly asked her to read when Mrs Duke gave a small sigh and stopped breathing.

Bertha closed her book, set the cat on her lap gently on the ground and went to take the old lady's hand. There was no pulse; she had known there wouldn't be.

She laid Mrs Duke's hands tidily in her lap and went into the tiny hall to where the doctor had left a portable phone, saying casually that she might need it and giving her a number to call. She hadn't thought much about it at the time, but now she blessed him for being thoughtful. She dialled the number—the clinic—and heard his quiet voice answer.

'Mrs Duke.' She tried to keep her voice steady.

'Please would you come quickly? She has just died…'

'Five minutes. Are you all right, Bertha?'

'Me? Yes, thank you. Only, please come…' Her voice wobbled despite her efforts.

It seemed less than five minutes until he opened the door and gave her a comforting pat on the shoulder as he went past her into the living room to examine Mrs Duke. He bent his great height over her for a few minutes and then straightened up.

'Exactly as she would have wished,' he said. 'In her own home and listening to one of her favourite stories.'

He looked at Bertha's pale face. 'Sit down while I get this sorted out.'

She sat with the two cats crouching on her lap—they were aware that something wasn't quite right—while he rang the clinic, and presently a pleasant elderly woman came and the doctor picked up Mrs Duke and carried her into her poky bedroom.

'I'll take you home,' he told Bertha. 'It's been a shock. I'm sorry you had to be here.'

'I'm not. I'm glad. If Mrs Duke didn't know anything about it… The cats—we can't just leave them.' She stroked their furry heads. 'I'd have them, only I don't think my stepmother…'

'I'll take them. There's room for them at my flat and Freddie will enjoy their company—my dog.'

'Mrs Duke would be glad of that; she loved them.' Bertha put the pair gently down and got to her feet. 'I could go by bus. I expect there's a lot for you to do.'

'Time enough for that. Come along.' He glanced at his watch. 'You need a cup of tea.'

'Please don't bother.' Two tears trickled slowly down her cheeks. 'It doesn't seem right to be talking about tea...'

'If Mrs Duke were here it would be the first thing that she would demand. Be happy for her, Bertha, for this is exactly what she wished for.'

Bertha sniffed, blew her nose and mopped up her tears. 'Yes, of course. Sorry. I'll come now. You're sure about the cats?'

'Yes. Wait while I have a word with Mrs Tyler.' He went into the bedroom and presently came out of it again, and whisked Bertha into the car.

He stopped the car in a side-street close to Oxford Street and ushered her into a small café where he sat her down at a table, ordered a pot of tea and took a seat opposite her.

'There is no need to say anything to your stepmother for the moment. It so happens that a nursery school I know of needs someone to read to the children. Would you consider doing that? The times may be different, but I'm sure I can explain that to Mrs Soames. Will you leave it to me? You will want to come to the funeral, won't you? Will you phone my rooms—tomorrow evening? Can you do that?'

'Well, I take my stepmother's dog for a walk every evening—I could go to the phone box; it's not far...'

'Splendid.' His smile was kind. 'Now, drink your tea and I'll take you home.' He added casually, 'I don't think there is any need to say anything to your stepmother about your change of job or Mrs Duke's death, do you?' He gave her a sidelong glance. 'I can explain that it will suit everyone concerned if the times are changed.'

'If you wouldn't mind. I don't think my stepmother would notice. I mean...'

'I know what you mean, Bertha.' His quiet voice reassured her.

The funeral was to be on Wednesday, she was told when she telephoned the following evening on her walk, and if she went as usual to the doctor's rooms she would be driven to Mrs Duke's flat. 'And as regards Monday,' went on the doctor, 'come at the usual time and I'll take you along to the nursery school so that you can meet everyone and arrange your hours.'

As she went back into the house she met Clare

in the hall, dressed to go out for the evening. She twirled round, showing off the short silky frock.

'Do you like it, Bertha? It shows off my legs very well, doesn't it? It's a dinner party at the Ritz.' She smiled her charming smile. 'I might as well have as much fun as possible before I settle down and become a fashionable doctor's wife.'

She danced off and Bertha took the dog to the kitchen. Was that why the doctor was being so kind to her, finding her work to fill her empty days? To please Clare, with whom he was in love? Well, who wouldn't be? reflected Bertha. Clare was so very pretty and such fun to be with.

She was surprised that her stepmother had had no objection to her changing the hours of her reading, but the doctor, driving her to the funeral, observed that there had been no trouble about it. 'Indeed, Mrs Soames seemed pleased that you have an outside interest.'

It was a remark which surprised Bertha, since her stepmother had evinced no interest in her comings and goings. It was a thought which she kept to herself.

A surprisingly large number of people were in the church. It seemed that Mrs Duke while alive had had few friends, but now even mere acquaintances crowded into the church and returned to her flat, filling it to overflowing while her nephew, a young man who had come from Sheffield with his wife, offered tea and meat-paste sandwiches.

Bertha, in the habit of making herself useful, filled the teacups and cut more bread and listened to the cheerful talk. Mrs Duke was being given a splendid send-off, and there had been a nice lot of flowers at the funeral.

'Aunty left her bits and pieces to me,' said her nephew, coming into the kitchen to make another pot of tea, 'as well as a bit in the Post Office. She 'as two cats too—I'll 'ave ter 'ave 'em destroyed. We've got a dog at home.'

'No need. Dr Hay-Smythe has taken them to his home.'

'Up ter 'im. 'E did a good job looking after Aunty.'

The doctor came in search of her presently. 'I think we might leave—I'll get someone to take over from you. Did you get a cup of tea?'

She shook her head. 'It doesn't matter.'

He smiled. 'It's a powerful brew. Wait there while I get someone…'

Mrs Tyler came back with him. 'Off you go, dearie. Everyone'll be here for another few hours and you've done more than your fair share. It was good of you and the doctor to come.'

'I liked Mrs Duke,' said Bertha.

'So did I. She'd have enjoyed this turn-out.'

'Are you expected home?' asked the doctor as he drove away.

'My stepmother and Clare are at a picture gallery and then going to have drinks with some friends. I expect you're busy—if you'd drop me off at a bus stop...'

'And then what will you do?' he wanted to know.

'Why, catch a bus, of course,' said Bertha in her practical way. 'And have a cup of tea when I get home.'

'Someone will have it ready for you?'

'Well, no. Crook's got the afternoon off and so has Daisy—she's the housemaid—and Cook will have her feet up—her bunions, you know.'

'In that case we'll have tea at my place.'

'It's very kind of you to ask me, but really you don't have to be polite. I've taken up a lot of your time, and you must have an awful lot to do.'

He spoke testily. 'Bertha, stop being so apologetic. If you don't wish to have tea with me say so. If not, come back with me and discuss the funeral over tea and toast.'

She said indignantly, 'I'm not being apologetic.' Her voice rose slightly. 'I don't care to be—to be...'

'Pitied? The last thing you can expect from me, my girl.'

He stopped outside his rooms and got out to

open her door. She looked up at him as she got out and found herself smiling.

Cully had the door open before they had reached it. He was introduced to Bertha and offered her a dignified bow before opening the sitting-room door.

'We would like tea, Cully,' said the doctor. 'Earl Grey and hot buttered toast—and if you can find a few cakes?'

'Certainly, sir. Shall I take the young lady's coat?'

He shuddered inwardly at the sight of the garish dress, but his face was inscrutable; he had until now had a poor opinion of any young ladies his master had brought home from time to time for the occasional drink or lunch, but this one was different, never mind the horrible garment she was wearing. He glided away to arrange cakes on a plate. Made by himself, of course. He didn't trust cakes bought in a shop.

Bertha, happily unaware of Cully's thoughts, went into the sitting room with the doctor to be greeted by Freddie before he went to his master's side.

'How very convenient,' said Bertha, 'having your home over your consulting rooms. I didn't know you lived here.'

She gently rubbed Freddie's head and looked around her. The room was very much to her

taste—a pleasing mixture of comfortable chairs
and sofas and antique wall cabinets, lamp-tables, a
magnificent Georgian rent table under the window
and a giltwood mirror over the fireplace. That was
Georgian too, she was sure.

She gave a little sigh of pleasure. 'This is a
beautiful room,' she told him gravely.

'I'm glad you like it. Do sit down.' He offered
her a small bergère, with upholstery matching the
mulberry brocade curtains, and took an armchair
opposite her. When her eyes darted to the long-
case clock as it chimed the hour of four, he said
soothingly, 'Don't worry. I'll see that you get back
home before anyone else.'

Cully came in then with a laden tray. He sat
everything out on a low table between them and
slid away, but not before he had taken a good look
at Bertha—nicely contrived from under lowered
lids. His first impressions had been good ones, he
decided.

Bertha made a good tea; she was hungry and
Cully's dainty sandwiches and little cakes were delicious. Sitting there in the quiet, restful room with
the doctor, whom she trusted and thought of as a
friend, she was content and happy, and if their conversation dealt entirely with the visits she was to
make to the nursery school she had no quarrel with
that. She had been reminded so often by her stepmother and Clare that she was a dull companion

and quite lacking in charm that she would have
been surprised if the doctor had been anything else
but briskly businesslike.

She was to go each morning from eleven o'clock
until half past twelve, if that suited her, he told
her, and she agreed at once. It might be a bit awkward sometimes, if she was needed to take the dog
out or to go to the shops on some errand for her
stepmother, but she would worry about that if and
when it happened; there was no need to tell him.

'There are any number of books there; the children are various ages—two years to around four or
five. You do understand that you need only read
to them? There are plenty of helpers to do the necessary chores.'

'I think I shall like it very much.' Bertha smiled.
'Every day, too…'

He took her home presently, waiting until she
had gone inside and then poked her head round the
front door to tell him that no one was home.

Beyond telling Bertha how fortunate she was that
Dr Hay-Smythe had found her something to do,
her stepmother asked no questions. It was incon-
venient that Bertha had to go each morning, of
course, but since he was almost a friend of the
family—indeed, almost more than that—she com-
plied. 'Clare is quite sure that he's in love with

her, so of course we would wish to do anything to oblige him in any way.'

So on Monday morning Bertha set off to go to the doctor's rooms. She was to go there first, he'd told her. The nursery school wasn't far from them and she would be shown the way and introduced to the matron who ran the place. She wasn't to feel nervous about going, for Matron already knew that she would be coming.

Mrs Taylor was at the rooms and greeted her with a friendly smile. 'Just a minute while I get Dr Hay-Smythe—he's in the garden with that dog of his.' She picked up the phone as she spoke, and a few minutes later he came in.

'I'll walk round with you, Bertha.' He glanced at his watch. 'I've time enough.'

She went with him down into the street and skipped along beside him to keep up.

'You can take a bus to the corner,' he told her. 'Go straight there after today.'

He turned down a narrow street and then turned again into a cul-de-sac lined with narrow, rather shabby houses. Halfway down he mounted the steps to a front door, rang the bell and then walked in.

The hall was rather bare, but the walls were a cheerful yellow and there was matting on the floor and a bowl of flowers on a table against the wall. The woman who came to meet them was small and stout with a jolly face and small bright eyes. She greeted the doctor like an old friend and looked at Bertha.

'So you're to be our reader,' she said, and shook hands. 'We are so glad to have you—we need all the help we can get. Come and see some of the children.'

She opened the door into a large, airy room full of children and several younger women. 'Of course, you won't be reading to them all,' she explained, 'but I've picked out those who will understand you, more or less. They love the sound of a voice, you know...'

They were in the centre of the room now with children all around them. 'We have children with special needs—three who are blind, several who had brain damage at birth and quite a few physically disabled...'

The doctor was watching Bertha's face. It showed surprise, compassion and a serene acceptance. Perhaps it had been unkind of him not to have told her, but he had wanted to see how she would react and she had reacted just as he had felt sure she would—with kindness, concern and not a trace of repugnance.

She looked at him and smiled. 'I'm going to like coming here,' she told him. 'Thank you for getting me the job.' She turned to the matron. 'I do hope I'll do...'

'Of course you will, my dear. Come along and take your jacket off and we'll get you settled.'

Bertha put out a hand to the doctor. 'I dare say I shan't see you again—well, perhaps when you come to see Clare, but you know what I mean. I can't thank you enough for your kindness.'

The doctor shook her hand in his large, firm one. 'Probably we shall see each other here occasionally. I come quite often to see the children.'

He went away then, and Bertha was led away by the matron, introduced to the other helpers and presently began to read to the circle of children assembled round her chair. It was an out-of-date book—an old fairy tale collection—and she started with the first story.

It wasn't going to be straightforward reading; she was interrupted frequently by eager little voices wanting her to read certain parts again, and some of them needed to have parts of the story explained to them, but after a time she got the hang of it and by half past twelve she and the children understood each other very well. She would do better tomorrow, she promised herself, going home to a solitary lunch, since her stepmother and Clare were out.

Within a few days Bertha had found her feet. It was a challenging job but she found it rewarding; the children were surprisingly happy, though sometimes difficult and frequently frustrated. They were lovable, though, and Bertha, lacking love in her own home, had plenty of that to offer.

At the end of two weeks she realised that she was happy, despite the dull life she led at home. Her stepmother still expected her to run errands, walk the dog and fetch and carry for her, so that she had little time to call her own. She was glad of that, really, as it gave her less time to think about Dr Hay-Smythe, for she had quickly discovered that she missed him.

She supposed that if Clare were to marry him—and, from what her stepsister said occasionally, Bertha thought that it was very likely—she would see him from time to time. He had been to the house once or twice, and Clare would recount their evenings together at great length, making no attempt to hide the fact that she had made up her mind to marry him.

When Bertha had asked her if she loved him, Clare had laughed. 'Of course not, but he's exactly what I want. Plenty of money, a handsome husband, and a chance to get away from home. Oh, I like him well enough...'

Bertha worried a lot about that; it spoilt her happiness. Dr Hay-Smythe wasn't the right husband for Clare. On the other hand, being in love with someone wasn't something one could arrange to suit oneself, and if he loved Clare perhaps it wouldn't matter.

It was towards the middle of the third week of her visits to the nursery school that Clare unexpectedly asked her to go shopping with her in the afternoon. 'I've some things I simply must buy and Mother wants the car, and I hate taxis on my own. You'll have to come.'

They set out after lunch, and since it had been raining, and was threatening to do so again, Crook hailed a taxi. Clare was in good spirits and disposed to be friendly.

'It's time you had something decent to wear,' she said surprisingly. 'There's that jersey two-piece of mine—I never liked it; it's a ghastly colour—you can have that.'

'I don't think I want it if it's a ghastly colour, Clare. Thank you all the same.'

'Oh, the colour is ghastly on *me*. I dare say you'll look all right in it.' She glanced at Bertha. 'You'd better take it. Mother won't buy you anything until Father gets home, and he's been delayed so you'll have to wait for it.'

Bertha supposed that the jersey two-piece wouldn't be any worse than the lime-green outfits and there was no one to see her in it anyway. She wondered silently if there would ever be a chance for her to earn some money. She was a voluntary worker, but if she worked longer hours perhaps she could ask to be paid? She wouldn't want much.

The idea cheered her up, so that she was able to stand about patiently while Clare tried on dresses and then finally bought a pair of Italian shoes—white kid with high heels and very intricate straps. Bertha, watching them being fitted, was green with envy; she had pretty feet and ankles, and Clare's were by no means perfect. The shoes were on the wrong feet, she reflected in a rare fit of ill-humour.

The afternoon had cleared. Clare gave Bertha the shoes to carry and said airily that they would walk home. 'We can always pick up a taxi if we get tired,' she declared. 'We'll cut through here.'

The street was a quiet one, empty of traffic and people. At least, it was until they were halfway down it. The elderly lady on the opposite pavement was walking slowly, carrying a plastic bag and an umbrella, with her handbag dangling from one arm, so she had no hands free to defend herself when, apparently from nowhere, two youths leapt at her from a narrow alleyway. They pushed her to the ground and one of them hit her as she tried to keep a hand on her bag.

Clare stopped suddenly. 'Quick, we must run for it. They'll be after us if they see us. Hurry, can't you?'

Bertha took no notice. She pushed away Clare's hands clinging to her arm, ran across the street and swiped at one of the youths with the plastic bag containing Clare's new shoes. It caught him on the shins and he staggered and fell. She swung the bag again, intent on hitting the other youth. The bag split this time and the shoes flew into the gutter.

Confronted by a virago intent on hurting them, the pair scrambled to their feet and fled, dropping the lady's handbag as they went. Short of breath and shaking with fright, Bertha knelt down by the old lady.

'My purse—my pension...' The elderly face was white with fear and worry. It was bruised, too.

'It's all right,' said Bertha. 'They dropped your handbag. I'll get it for you. But, first of all, are you hurt?'

Before the old lady could answer, Clare hissed into Bertha's ear, 'My shoes—my lovely new shoes. You've ruined them. I'll never forgive you!'

'Oh, bother your shoes,' said Bertha. 'Go and bang on someone's door and get an ambulance.'

Just for once, Clare, speechless at Bertha's brisk orders, did as she was told.

She was back presently, and there were people with her. Bertha, doing her best to make the old lady as comfortable as possible, listened with half an ear to her stepsister's voice.

'Two huge men,' said Clare, in what Bertha always thought of as her little-girl voice. 'They ran at this poor lady and knocked her down. I simply rushed across the street and hit them with a shopping bag—one of them fell over and they ran away then.' She gave a little laugh. 'I've never been so scared in my life...'

'Very plucky, if I might say so,' said a voice.

Another voice asked, 'You're not hurt, young lady? It was a brave thing to do.'

'Well, one doesn't think of oneself,' murmured Clare. 'And luckily my sister came to help me once the men had gone.'

The old lady stared up at Bertha's placid face. 'That's a pack of lies,' she whispered. 'It was you; I saw you...' She closed her eyes tiredly. 'I shall tell someone...'

'It doesn't matter,' said Bertha. 'All that matters is that you're safe. Here is your handbag, and the purse is still inside.'

She got to her feet as the ambulance drew up and the few people who had gathered to see what was amiss gave her sidelong glances with no sign of friendliness; she could read their thoughts— leaving her pretty sister to cope with those violent men... Luckily there were still brave girls left in this modern day and age of violence...

Bertha told herself that it didn't matter; they were strangers and never likely to see her again. She wondered what Clare would do next—beg a lift from someone, most likely.

There was no need for that, however.

By good fortune—or was it bad fortune?—Dr Hay-Smythe, on his way from somewhere or other, had seen the little group as he drove past. He stopped, reversed neatly and got out of his car. Clare, with a wistful little cry, exactly right for the occasion, ran to meet him.

# CHAPTER THREE

'OLIVER!' cried Clare, in what could only be described as a brave little voice. 'Thank heaven you're here.' She waved an arm towards the ambulancemen loading the old lady onto a stretcher. 'This poor old woman—there were two enormous men attacking her. She's been hurt—she might have been killed—but I ran as fast as I could and threw my bag at them and they ran away.'

The onlookers, gathering close, murmured admiringly. 'Proper brave young lady,' said one.

'Oh, no,' Clare said softly. 'Anyone would have done the same.' She had laid a hand on the doctor's arm and now looked up into his face.

He wasn't looking at her. He was watching the stretcher being lifted into the ambulance. The old lady was saying something to Bertha, who had whipped a bit of paper and pencil from her bag and was writing something down.

He removed Clare's hand quite gently. 'I should just take a look,' he observed.

He spoke to the ambulance driver and then bent over the old lady, giving Bertha a quick smile as he did so. 'Can I help in any way? I'm told there's nothing broken, but you had better have a check-up at the hospital.'

The shrewd old eyes studied his face. 'You're a doctor? Don't you listen to that girl's tale. Not a word of truth in it. Seen it with my own eyes— tried to run away, she did. It was this child who tackled those thugs—twice her size too.' She gave a weak snort of indignation. 'Mad as fire because her shoes had been spoilt. Huh!'

'Thank you for telling me. Do we have your name? Is there anyone who should be told?'

'This young lady's seen to that for me, bless her. Gets things done while others talk.'

'Indeed she does.' He took her hand. 'You'll be all right now.'

He went back to the driver and presently, when the ambulance had been driven away, he joined Bertha. 'Let me have her name and address, will you? I'll check on her later today. Now I'll drive you both home.'

Clare had joined them. 'What was all that about? You don't need to bother any more; she'll be looked after at the hospital. I feel awfully odd—it was a shock…'

'I'll drive you both back home. I dare say you may like to go straight to bed, Clare.'

Clare jumped into the car. 'No, no—I'm not such a weakling as all that, Oliver. I dare say Bertha would like to lie down for a bit, though—

she was so frightened.' She turned her head to look at Bertha on the back seat, who looked out of the window and didn't answer.

The doctor didn't say anything either, so Clare went on uncertainly, 'Well, of course, it was enough to scare the wits out of anyone, wasn't it?'

No one answered that either. Presently she said pettishly, 'I had a pair of new shoes—wildly expensive—they've been ruined.' Quite forgetting her role of brave girl, she turned on Bertha. 'You'll have to pay for them, Bertha. Throwing them around like that—' She stopped, aware that she had let the cat out of the bag. 'What was the good of flinging the bag at those men when they had already run away?'

'I'm sure you can buy more shoes,' said the doctor blandly. 'And what is a pair of shoes compared with saving an old lady from harm?'

He glanced in his mirror, caught Bertha's eye and smiled at her, and lowered an eyelid in an unmistakable wink.

It gave her a warm glow. Never mind that there would be some hard words when she got home; she had long since learned to ignore them. He had believed the old lady and she had the wit to see that he wouldn't mention it—it would make it so much worse for her and would probably mean the end of her job at the nursery school. If any special attention from him were to come to Clare's or her stepmother's notice, they would find a way to make sure that she never saw him again...

The doctor stopped the car before their door, and Clare said coaxingly, 'Take me out to dinner this evening, Oliver? I do need cheering up after all I've just gone through. Somewhere quiet where we can talk?'

He had got out to open her door and now turned to do the same for Bertha. 'Impossible, I'm afraid. I've a meeting at seven o'clock which will last for hours—perhaps at the weekend...'

He closed the car door. 'I suggest that you both have an early night. If there is any news of the old lady I'll let you have it. I shall be seeing her later this evening. Bertha, if you will give me her address, I'll see that her family are told.'

She handed it over with a murmured thank-you, bade him goodbye and started up the steps to the door, leaving Clare to make a more protracted leavetaking—something which he nipped in the bud with apparent reluctance.

Clare's charm turned to cold fury as they entered the house. 'You'll pay for this,' she stormed. 'Those shoes cost the earth. Now I've nothing to wear with that new dress...'

Bertha said matter-of-factly, 'Well, I can't pay for them, can I? I haven't any money. And you've dozens of shoes.' She looked at Clare's furious face. 'Are they really more important than helping someone in a fix?' She wanted to know. 'And what a lot of fibs you've told everyone. I must say you looked the part.'

She stopped then, surprised at herself, but not nearly as surprised as Clare. 'How dare you?' Clare snapped. 'How dare you talk to me like that?'

'Well, it's the truth, isn't it?' asked Bertha placidly. 'But, don't worry, I shan't give you away.'

'No one would believe you...'

'Probably not.' Bertha went up to her room, leaving Clare fuming.

The full weight of her stepmother's displeasure fell upon her when she went downstairs presently. She was most ungrateful, careless and unnaturally mean towards her stepsister, who had behaved with the courage only to be expected of her. Bertha should be bitterly ashamed of herself. 'I had intended to take you to a charity coffee morning at Lady Forde's, but I shall certainly not do so now,' she finished.

Bertha, allowing the harsh voice to wash over her head, heaved a sigh of relief; the last time she had been taken there she had ended up making herself useful, helping Lady Forde's meek companion hand round the coffee and cakes. She looked down at her lap and didn't say a word. What would be the use?

\*    \*    \*

She would have been immensely cheered if she had known of the doctor's efforts on her behalf. There had to be a way, he reflected, sitting in his sitting room with Freddie at his feet, in which he could give Bertha a treat. It seemed to him that she had no fun at all—indeed, was leading an unhappy life.

'She deserves better,' he told Freddie, who yawned. 'Properly dressed and turned out, she might stand a chance of attracting some young man. She has beautiful eyes, and I don't know another girl who would have held her tongue as she did this afternoon.'

It was much later, after Cully had gone to his bed and the house was quiet, that he knew what he would do. Well satisfied, he settled Freddie in his basket in the kitchen and went to bed himself.

The doctor waited another two days before calling at Mrs Soames's house. He had satisfied himself that Bertha was still going to the nursery. Matron had been enthusiastic about her and assured him that there had been no question of her leaving, so he was able to dispel the nagging thought that her stepmother might have shown her anger by forbidding her to go.

He chose a time when he was reasonably sure that they would all be at home and gave as his excuse his concern as to whether the two girls had got over their unfortunate experience. All three ladies were in the drawing room—something which pleased him, for if Bertha wasn't there, there was always the chance that she would hear nothing of his plans.

Mrs Soames rose to meet him. 'My dear Oliver, most kind of you to call—as you see, we are sitting quietly at home. Dear Clare is somewhat shocked still.'

'I'm sorry to hear it,' said the doctor, shaking Clare's hand and giving Bertha a smiling nod. 'Perhaps I can offer a remedy—both for her and for Bertha, who must also be just as upset.'

Mrs Soames looked surprised. 'Bertha? I hardly think so. She isn't in the least sensitive.'

The doctor looked grave and learned. He said weightily, 'Nevertheless, I think that both young ladies would benefit from my plan.'

His bedside manner, reflected Bertha, and very impressive and effective too, for her stepmother nodded and said, 'Of course. I bow to your wisdom, Oliver.'

'Most fortunately I am free tomorrow. I should be delighted if I might drive them into the country for the day, away from London. To slow down one's lifestyle once in a while is necessary, especially when one has had a shock such as Clare had.' He looked at Bertha. 'And I am sure that

Bertha must have been upset. I haven't had the opportunity to ask her—'

'There's no need,' Clare interrupted him hastily. 'I'm sure she needs a break just as I do. We'd love to come with you, Oliver. Where shall we go?'

'How about a surprise? Is ten o'clock too early for you?'

'No, no. Not a minute too early.' Clare was at her most charming, and then, as he got up to go, she said suddenly, 'But of course Bertha won't be able to go with us—she reads to old ladies or something every morning.'

'Tomorrow is Saturday,' the doctor reminded her gently. 'I doubt if she does that at the weekends.' He glanced at Bertha. 'Is that not so, Bertha?'

Bertha murmured an agreement and saw the flash of annoyance on Clare's face. All of a sudden she was doubtful as to whether a day spent in the company of Clare and the doctor would be as pleasant as it sounded.

After he had gone, Clare said with satisfaction, 'You haven't anything to wear, Bertha. I hope Oliver won't feel embarrassed. It's a great pity that you have to come with us. You could have refused.'

'I shall enjoy a day out,' said Bertha calmly, 'and I shall wear the jersey two-piece you handed down to me. I'll have to take it in...'

Clare jumped up. 'You ungrateful girl. That outfit cost a lot of money.'

'It's a ghastly colour,' said Bertha equably, and went away to try it on. It was indeed a garment which Clare should never have bought—acid-yellow, and it needed taking in a good deal.

'Who cares?' said Bertha defiantly to the kitchen cat, who had followed her upstairs, and began to sew—a tricky business since her eyes were full of tears. To be with the doctor again would be, she had to admit, the height of happiness, but she very much doubted if he would feel the same. He was far too well-mannered to comment upon the two-piece—probably he would be speechless when he saw it—but it would be nice to spend a day with him wearing an outfit which was the right colour and which fitted.

'I suppose I am too thin,' she observed to the cat, pinning darts and cobbling them up. The sleeves were a bit too long—she would have to keep pushing them up—and the neck was too low. Clare liked low necks so that she could display her plump bosom, but Bertha, who had a pretty bosom of her own, stitched it up to a decent level and hoped that no one would notice.

Dr Hay-Smythe noticed it at once, even though half-blinded by the acid-yellow. An appalling outfit, he reflected, obviously hastily altered, for it didn't fit anywhere it should and the colour did nothing for Bertha's ordinary features and light brown hair. He found that he was full of rage at her treatment, although he allowed nothing of that to show. He wished her good morning and talked pleasantly to Mrs Soames while they waited for Clare.

She came at last, with little cries of regret at keeping him waiting. 'I wanted to look as nice as possible for you, Oliver,' she said with a little laugh. And indeed she did look nice—in blue and white wool, simply cut and just right for a day in the country. She had a navy shoulder-bag and matching shoes with high heels. The contrast between the two girls was cruel.

The doctor said breezily, 'Ah, here you are at last. I was beginning to think that you had changed your mind!' He smiled a little. 'Found someone younger and more exciting with whom to spend the day.'

This delighted Clare. 'There isn't anyone more exciting than you, Oliver,' she cooed, and Bertha looked away, feeling sick and wishing that the day was over before it had begun.

Of course Clare got into the seat beside Oliver, leaving him to usher Bertha into the back of the car where Freddie, delighted to have company, greeted her with pleasure.

Clare, turning round to stare, observed tartly,

'Oh, you've brought a dog.' And then said, with a little laugh, 'He'll be company for Bertha.'

'Freddie goes wherever I go when it's possible. He sits beside me on long journeys and is a delightful companion.'

'Well, now you have me,' declared Clare. 'I'm a delightful companion too!'

A remark which the doctor apparently didn't hear.

He drove steadily towards the western suburbs, apparently content to listen to Clare's chatter, and when he was finally clear of the city he turned off the main road and slowed the car as they reached the countryside. They were in Hertfordshire now, bypassing the towns, taking minor roads through the woods and fields and going through villages, peaceful under the morning sun. At one of these he stopped at an inn.

'Coffee?' he asked, and got out to open Clare's door and then usher Bertha and Freddie out of the car.

The inn was old and thatched and cosy inside. The doctor asked for coffee, then suggested, 'You two girls go ahead. I'll take Freddie for a quick run while the coffee's fetched.'

The ladies' was spotlessly clean, but lacked the comforts of its London counterparts. Clare, doing her face in front of the only mirror, said crossly, 'He might have stopped at a decent hotel—this is pretty primitive. I hope we shall lunch somewhere more civilised.'

'I like it,' said Bertha. 'I like being away from London. I'd like to live in the country.'

Clare didn't bother to reply, merely remarking as they went to join the doctor that the yellow jersey looked quite frightful. 'When I see you in it,' said Clare, 'I can see just how ghastly it is!'

It was an opinion shared by the doctor as he watched them cross the bar to join him at a table by the window, but nothing could dim the pleasure in Bertha's face, and, watching it, he hardly noticed the outfit.

'The coffee was good. I'm surprised,' said Clare. 'I mean, in a place like this you don't expect it, do you?'

'Why not?' The doctor was at his most genial. 'The food in some of these country pubs is as good or better than that served in some of the London restaurants. No dainty morsels in a pretty pattern on your plate, but just steak and kidney pudding and local vegetables, or sausages and mash with apple pie for a pudding.'

Clare looked taken aback. If he intended giving her sausages and mash for lunch she would demand to be taken home. 'Where are we lunching?' she asked.

'Ah, wait and see!'

Bertha had drunk her coffee almost in silence,

with Freddie crouching under the table beside her, nudging her gently for a bit of biscuit from time to time. She hoped that they would lunch in a country pub—sausages and mash would be nice, bringing to mind the meal she and the doctor had eaten together. Meeting him had changed her life...

They drove on presently into Buckinghamshire, still keeping to the country roads. It was obvious that the doctor knew where he was going. Bertha stopped herself from asking him; it might spoil whatever surprise he had in store for them.

It was almost noon when they came upon a small village—a compact gathering of Tudor cottages with a church overlooking them from the brow of a low hill.

Bertha peered and said, 'Oh, this is delightful. Where are we?'

'This is Wing—'

'Isn't there a hotel?' asked Clare. 'We're not going to stop here, are we?' She had spoken sharply. 'It's a bit primitive, isn't it?' She saw his lifted eyebrows. 'Well, no, not primitive, perhaps, but you know what I mean, Oliver. Or is there one of those country-house restaurants tucked away out of sight?'

He only smiled and turned the car through an open wrought-iron gate. The drive was short, and at its end was a house—not a grand house, one might call it a gentleman's residence—sitting squarely amidst trees and shrubs with a wide lawn before it edged by flowerbeds. Bertha, examining it from the car, thought that it must be Georgian, with its Palladian door with a pediment above, its many paned windows and tall chimneystacks.

It wasn't just a lovely old house, it was a home; there were long windows, tubs of japonica on either side of the door, the bare branches of Virginia creeper rioting over its walls and, watching them from a wrought-iron sill above a hooded bay window, a majestic cat with a thick orange coat. Bertha saw all this as Clare got out, the latter happy now at the sight of a house worthy of her attention and intent on making up for her pettishness.

'I suppose we are to lunch here?' she asked as the doctor opened Bertha's door and she and Freddie tumbled out.

His 'yes' was noncommittal.

'It isn't a hotel, is it?' asked Bertha. 'It's someone's home. It's quite beautiful.'

'I'm glad you like it, Bertha. It is my home. My mother will be delighted to have you both as her guests for lunch.'

'Yours?' queried Clare eagerly. 'As well as your flat in town? I suppose your mother will live here until you want it for yourself—when you marry?' She gave him one of her most charming smiles, which he ignored.

'Your mother doesn't mind?' asked Bertha. 'If we are unexpected...'

'You're not. I phoned her yesterday. She is glad to welcome you—she is sometimes a little lonely since my father died.'

'Oh, I'm sorry.' Bertha's plain face was full of sympathy.

'Thank you. Shall we go indoors?'

The house door opened under his hand and he ushered them into the wide hall with its oak floor and marble-topped console table flanked by cane and walnut chairs. There was a leather-covered armchair in one corner too, the repository of a variety of coats, jackets, walking sticks, dog leads and old straw hats, giving the rather austere grandeur of the hall a pleasantly lived-in look. The doctor led the way past the oak staircase with its wrought-iron balustrade at the back of the hall and opened a small door.

'Mother will be in the garden,' he observed. 'We can go through the kitchen.'

The kitchen was large with a vast dresser loaded with china against one wall, an Aga stove and a scrubbed table ringed by Windsor chairs at its centre. Two women looked up as they went in.

'Master Oliver, good morning to you, sir—and the two young ladies.'

The speaker was short and stout and wrapped

around by a very white apron. The doctor crossed the room and kissed her cheek.

'Meg, how nice to see you again.' He looked across at the second woman, who was a little younger and had a severe expression. 'And Dora—you're both well? Good. Clare, Bertha—this is Meg, our cook, and Dora, who runs the house.'

Clare nodded and said, 'hello,' but Bertha smiled and shook hands.

'What a heavenly kitchen.' Her lovely eyes were sparkling with pleasure. 'It's a kind of haven...' She blushed because she had said something silly, but Meg and Dora were smiling.

'That it is, miss—specially now in the winter of an evening. Many a time Mr Oliver's popped in here to beg a slice of dripping toast.'

He smiled. 'Meg, you are making my mouth water. We had better go and find my mother. We'll see you before we go.'

Clare had stood apart, tapping a foot impatiently, but as they went through the door into the garden beyond she slipped an arm through the doctor's.

'I love your home,' she told him, 'and your lovely old-fashioned servants.'

'They are our friends as well, Clare. They have been with us for as long as I can remember.'

The garden behind the house was large and rambling, with narrow paths between the flowerbeds and flowering shrubs. Freddie rushed ahead, and they heard his barking echoed by a shrill yapping.

'My mother will be in the greenhouses.' The doctor had disengaged his arm from Clare's in order to lead the way, and presently they went through a ramshackle door in a high brick wall and saw the greenhouses to one side of the kitchen garden.

Bertha, lingering here and there to look at neatly tended borders and shrubs, saw that Clare's high heels were making heavy weather of the earth paths. Her clothes were exquisite, but here, in this country garden, they didn't look right. Bertha glanced down at her own person and had to admit that her own outfit didn't look right either. She hoped that the doctor's mother wasn't a follower of fashion like her stepmother.

She had no need to worry; the lady who came to meet them as the doctor opened the greenhouse door was wearing a fine wool skirt stained with earth and with bits of greenery caught up in it, and her blouse, pure silk and beautifully made, was almost covered by a misshapen cardigan of beige cashmere as stained as the skirt. She was wearing wellies and thick gardening gloves and looked, thought Bertha, exactly as the doctor's mother should look.

She wasn't quite sure what she meant by this, it was something that she couldn't put into words, but she knew instinctively that this elderly lady with her plain face and sweet expression was all that she would have wanted if her own mother had lived.

'My dear.' Mrs Hay-Smythe lifted up her face for her son's kiss. 'How lovely to see you—and these are the girls who had such an unpleasant experience the other day?'

She held out a hand, the glove pulled off. 'I'm delighted to meet you. You must tell me all about it, presently—I live such a quiet life here that I'm all agog to hear the details.'

'Oh, it was nothing, Mrs Hay-Smythe,' said Clare. 'I'm sure there are many more people braver than I. It is so kind of Oliver to bring us; I had no idea that he had such a beautiful home.'

Mrs Hay-Smythe looked a little taken aback, but she smiled and said, 'Well, yes, we're very happy to live here.'

She turned to Bertha. 'And you are Bertha?' Her smile widened and her blue eyes smiled too, never once so much as glancing at the yellow jersey. 'Forgive me that I am so untidy, but there is always work to do in the greenhouse. We'll go indoors and have a drink. Oliver will look after you while I tidy myself.'

They wandered back to the house—Clare ahead with the doctor, his mother coming slowly with Bertha, stopping to describe the bushes and flowers that would bloom in the spring as they went, Freddie and her small border terrier beside them.

'You are fond of gardening?' she wanted to know.

'Well, we live in a townhouse, you know. There's a gardener, and he comes once a week to see to the garden—but he doesn't grow things, just comes and digs up whatever's there and then plants the next lot. That's not really gardening. I'd love to have a packet of seeds and grow flowers, but I—I don't have much time.'

Mrs Hay-Smythe, who knew all about Bertha, nodded sympathetically. 'I expect one day you'll get the opportunity—when you marry, you know.'

'I don't really expect to marry,' said Bertha matter-of-factly. 'I don't meet many people and I'm plain.' She sounded quite cheerful and her hostess smiled.

'Well, as to that, I'm plain, my dear, and I was a middle daughter of six living in a remote vicarage. And that, I may tell you, was quite a handicap.'

They both laughed and Clare, standing waiting for them with the doctor, frowned. Just like Bertha to worm her way into their hostess's good books, she thought. Well, she would soon see about that.

As they went into the house she edged her way towards Mrs Hay-Smythe. 'This is such a lovely house. I do hope there will be time for you to take

me round before we go back.' She remembered
that that would leave Bertha with Oliver, which
would never do. 'Bertha too, of course...'

Mrs Hay-Smythe had manners as beautiful as
her son's. 'I shall be delighted. But now I must go
and change. Oliver, give the girls a drink, will you?
I'll be ten minutes or so. We mustn't keep Meg
waiting.'

It seemed to Bertha that the doctor was perfectly
content to listen to Clare's chatter as she drank her
gin and lime, and his well-mannered attempts to
draw her into the conversation merely increased
her shyness. So silly, she reflected, sipping her
sherry, because when I'm with him and there's no
one else there I'm perfectly normal.

Mrs Hay-Smythe came back presently, wearing
a black and white dress, which, while being elegant, suited her age. A pity, thought Bertha, still
wrapped in thought, that her stepmother didn't
dress in a similar manner, instead of forcing herself
into clothes more suitable to a woman of half her
age. She was getting very mean and unkind, she
reflected.

Lunch eaten in a lovely panelled room with an
oval table and a massive sideboard of mahogany,
matching shield-back chairs and a number of por-
traits in heavy gilt frames on its walls, was simple
but beautifully cooked: miniature onion tarts dec-
orated with olives and strips of anchovy, grilled

trout with a pepper sauce and a green salad, followed by orange cream soufflés.

Bertha ate with unselfconscious pleasure and a good appetite and listened resignedly to Clare tell her hostess as she picked daintily at her food that she adored French cooking.

'We have a chef who cooks the most delicious food.' She gave one of her little laughs. 'I'm so fussy, I'm afraid. But I adore lobster, don't you? And those little tartlets with caviare…'

Mrs Hay-Smythe smiled and offered Bertha a second helping. Bertha, pink with embarrassment, accepted. So did the doctor and his mother, so that Clare was left to sit and look at her plate while the three of them ate unhurriedly.

They had coffee in the conservatory and soon the doctor said, 'We have a family pet at the bottom of the garden. Nellie the donkey. She enjoys visitors and Freddie is devoted to her. Shall we stroll down to see her?'

He smiled at Bertha's eager face and Freddie was already on his feet when Clare said quickly, 'Oh, but we are to see the house. I'm longing to go all over it.'

'In that case,' said Mrs Hay-Smythe in a decisive voice, 'you go on ahead to Nellie, Oliver, and take Bertha with you, and I'll take Clare to see a little of the house.' When Clare would have protested that perhaps, after all, she would rather see the donkey, Mrs Hay-Smythe said crisply, 'No, no, I mustn't disappoint you. We can join the others very shortly.'

She whisked Clare indoors and the doctor stood up. 'Come along, Bertha. We'll go to the kitchen and get a carrot...'

Meg and Dora were loading the dishwasher, and the gentle clatter of crockery made a pleasant background for the loud tick-tock of the kitchen clock and the faint strains of the radio. There was a tabby cat before the Aga, and the cat with the orange coat was sitting on the window-sill.

'Carrots?' said Meg. 'For that donkey of yours, Master Oliver? Pampered, that's what she is.' She smiled broadly at Bertha. 'Not but what she's an old pet, when all's said and done.'

Dora had gone to fetch the carrots and the doctor was sitting on the kitchen table eating a slice of the cake that was presumably for tea.

'I enjoyed my lunch,' said Bertha awkwardly. 'You must be a marvellous cook, Meg.'

'Lor' bless you, miss, anyone can cook who puts their mind to it.' But Meg looked pleased all the same.

The donkey was in a small orchard at the bottom of the large garden. She was an elderly beast who was pleased to see them; she ate the carrots and then trotted around a bit in a dignified way with a delighted Freddie.

The doctor, leaning on the gate to the orchard, looked sideways at Bertha. She was happy, her face full of contentment. She was happily oblivious of her startling outfit too—which was even more startling in the gentle surroundings.

Conscious that he was looking at her, she turned her head and their eyes met.

Good gracious, thought Bertha, I feel as if I've known him all my life, that I've been waiting for him...

Clare's voice broke the fragile thread which had been spun between them. 'There you are. Is this the donkey? Oliver, you do have a lovely house—your really ought to marry and share it with some-one.'

# CHAPTER FOUR

THEY didn't stay long in the orchard—Clare's high-heeled shoes sank into the ground at every step and her complaints weren't easily ignored. They sat in the conservatory again, and Clare told them amusing tales about her friends and detailed the plays she had recently seen and the parties she had attended.

'I scarcely have a moment to myself,' she declared on a sigh. 'You can't imagine how delightful a restful day here is.'

'You would like to live in the country?' asked Mrs Hay-Smythe.

'In a house like this? Oh, yes. One could run up to town whenever one felt like it—shopping and the theatre—and I dare say there are other people living around here…'

'Oh, yes.' Mrs Hay-Smythe spoke pleasantly. 'Oliver, will you ask Meg to bring tea out here?'

After tea they took their leave and got into the car, and were waved away by Mrs Hay-Smythe. Bertha waved back, taking a last look at the house she wasn't likely to see again but would never forget.

As for Mrs Hay-Smythe, she went to the kitchen, where she found Meg and Dora having their own tea. She sat down at the table with them and accepted a cup of strong tea with plenty of milk. Not her favourite brand, but she felt that she needed something with a bite to it.

'Well?' she asked.

'Since you want to know, ma'am,' said Meg, 'and speaking for the two of us, we just hope that the master isn't taken with that young lady what didn't eat her lunch. High and mighty, we thought—didn't we, Dora?'

'Let me put your minds at rest. This visit was made in order to give the other Miss Soames a day out, but to do so it was necessary to invite her stepsister as well.'

'Well, there,' said Dora. 'Like Cinderella. Such a nice quiet young lady too. Thanked you for her lunch, didn't she, Meg?'

'That she did, and not smarmy either. Fitted into the house very nicely too.'

'Yes, she did,' said Mrs Hay-Smythe thoughtfully. Bertha would make a delightful daughter-in-law, but Oliver had given no sign—he had helped her out of kindness but shown no wish to be in her company or even talk to her other than in a casual friendly way. 'A pity,' said Mrs Hay-Smythe, and with Flossie, her little dog, at her heels she went back to the greenhouse, where she put on a vast

apron and her gardening gloves and began work
again.

The doctor drove back the way they had come,
listening to Clare's voice and hardly hearing what
she was saying. Only when she said insistently,
'You will take me out to dinner this evening, won't
you, Oliver? Somewhere lively where we can
dance afterwards? It's been a lovely day, but after
all that rural quiet we could do with some town
life…'

'When we get back,' he said, 'I am going
straight to the hospital where I shall be for several
hours, and I have an appointment for eight o'clock
tomorrow morning. I am a working man, Clare.'

She pouted. 'Oh, Oliver, can't you forget the
hospital just for once? I was so sure you'd take me
out.'

'Quite impossible. Besides, I'm not a party man,
Clare.'

She touched his sleeve. 'I could change that for
you. At least promise you'll come to dinner one
evening? I'll tell Mother to give you a ring.'

He glanced in the side-mirror and saw that
Bertha was sitting with her arm round Freddie's
neck, looking out of the window. Her face was
turned away, but the back of her head looked sad.

He stayed only as long as good manners re-
quired when they reached the Soameses' house,

and when he had gone Clare threw her handbag down and flung herself into a chair.

Her mother asked sharply, 'Well, you had Oliver all to yourself—is he interested?'

'Well, of course he is. If only we hadn't taken Bertha with us...'

'She didn't interfere, I hope.'

'She didn't get the chance—she hardly spoke to him. I didn't give her the opportunity. She was with his mother most of the time.'

'What is Mrs Hay-Smythe like?'

'Oh, boring—talking about the garden and the Women's Institute and doing the flowers for the church. She was in the greenhouse when we got there. I thought she was one of the servants.'

'Not a lady?' asked her mother, horrified.

'Oh, yes, no doubt about that. Plenty of money too, I should imagine. The house is lovely—it would be a splendid country home for weekends if we could have a decent flat here.' She laughed. 'The best of both worlds.'

Bertha, in her room, changing out of the two-piece and getting into another of Clare's too-elaborate dresses, told the kitchen cat, who was enjoying a stolen hour or so on her bed, all about her day.

'I don't suppose Oliver will be able to withstand Clare for much longer—only I mustn't call him Oliver, must I? I'm not supposed to have more than a nodding acquaintance with him.' She sat down on the bed, the better to address her companion. 'I think that is what I must do in the future, just nod. I think about him too much and I miss him…'

She went to peer at her face in the mirror and nodded at its reflection. 'Plain as a pikestaff, my girl.'

Dinner was rather worse than usual, for there were no guests and that gave her stepmother and Clare the opportunity to criticise her behaviour during the day.

'Clare tells me that you spent too much time with Mrs Hay-Smythe…'

Bertha popped a morsel of fish into her mouth and chewed it. 'Well,' she said reasonably, 'what else was I to do? Clare wouldn't have liked it if I'd attached myself to Dr Hay-Smythe, and it would have looked very ill-mannered if I'd just gone off on my own.'

Mrs Soames glared, seeking for a quelling reply. 'Anyway, you should never have gone off with the doctor while Clare was in the house with his mother.'

'I enjoyed it. We talked about interesting things—the donkey and the orchard and the house.'

'He must have been bored,' said her stepmother crossly.

Bertha looked demure. 'Yes, I think that some of the time he was—very bored.'

Clare tossed her head. 'Not when he was with me,' she said smugly, but her mother shot Bertha a frowning look.

'I think you should understand, Bertha, that Dr Hay-Smythe is very likely about to propose marriage to your stepsister…'

'Has he said so?' asked Bertha composedly. She studied Mrs Soames, whose high colour had turned faintly purple.

'Certainly not, but one feels these things.' Mrs Soames pushed her plate aside. 'I am telling you this because I wish you to refuse any further invitations which the doctor may offer you—no doubt out of kindness.'

'Why?'

'There is an old saying—two is company, three is a crowd.'

'Oh, you don't want me to play gooseberry. I looked like one today in that frightful outfit Clare passed on to me.'

'You ungrateful—' began Clare, but was silenced by a majestic wave of her mother's hand.

'I cannot think what has come over you, Bertha. Presumably this day's outing has gone to your head. The two-piece Clare so kindly gave you is charming.'

'Then why doesn't she wear it?' asked Bertha,

feeling reckless. She wasn't sure what had come over her either, but she was rather enjoying it. 'I would like some new clothes of my own.'

Mrs Soames's bosom swelled alarmingly. 'That is enough, Bertha. I shall buy you something suitable when I have the leisure to arrange it. I think you had better have an early night, for you aren't yourself... The impertinence...'

'Is that what it is? It feels nice!' said Bertha.

She excused herself with perfect good manners and went up to her room. She lay in the bath for a long time, having a good cry but not sure why she was crying. At least, she had a vague idea at the back of her head as to why she felt lonely and miserable, but she didn't allow herself to pursue the matter. She got into bed and the cat curled up against her back, purring in a comforting manner, so that she was lulled into a dreamless sleep.

Her mother and Clare had been invited to lunch with friends who had a house near Henley. Bertha had been invited too, but she didn't know that. Mrs Soames had explained to their hosts that she had a severe cold in the head and would spend the day in bed.

Bertha was up early, escorting the cat back to her rightful place in the kitchen and making herself tea. She would have almost the whole day to herself; Crook was to have an afternoon off and

Cook's sister was coming to spend the day with her.

Mrs Soames found this quite satisfactory since Bertha could be served a cold lunch and get her own tea if Cook decided to walk down to the nearest bus stop with her sister. The daily maid never came on a Sunday.

All this suited Bertha; she drank her tea while the cat lapped milk, and decided what she would do with her day. A walk—a long walk. She would go to St James's Park and feed the ducks. She went back upstairs to dress and had almost finished breakfast when Clare joined her. Bertha said good morning and she got a sour look, which she supposed was only to be expected.

It was after eleven o'clock by the time Mrs Soames and Clare had driven away. Bertha, thankful that it was a dull, cold day, allowing her to wear the lime-green which she felt was slightly less awful than the two-piece, went to tell Crook that she might be late for lunch and ask him to leave it on a tray for her before he left the house and set out.

There wasn't a great deal of traffic in the streets, but there were plenty of people taking their Sunday walk as she neared the park. She walked briskly, her head full of daydreams, not noticing her surroundings until someone screamed.

A young woman was coming out of the park

gates pushing a pram—and running across the street into the path of several cars was a small boy. Bertha ran. She ran fast, unhampered by high heels and handbag, and plucked the child from the nearest car's wheels just before those same wheels bowled her over.

The child's safe, she thought hazily, aware that every bone in her body ached and that she was lying in a puddle of water, but somehow she felt too tired to get up. She felt hands and then heard voices, any number of them, asking if she were hurt.

'No—thank you,' said Bertha politely. 'Just aching a bit. Is that child OK?'

There was a chorus of 'yes', and somebody said that there was an ambulance coming. 'No need,' said Bertha, not feeling at all herself. 'If I could get up...'

'No, no,' said a voice. 'There may be broken bones...'

So she stayed where she was, listening to the voices; there seemed to be a great many people all talking at once. She was feeling sick now...

There were no broken bones, the ambulanceman assured her, but they laid her on a stretcher, popped her into the ambulance and bore her away to hospital. They had put a dressing on her leg without saying why.

The police were there by then, wanting to know her name and where she lived.

'Bertha Soames. But there is no one at home.'

Well, Cook was, but what could she do? Better keep quiet. Bertha closed her eyes, one of which was rapidly turning purple.

Dr Hay-Smythe, called down to the accident and emergency department to examine a severe head injury, paused to speak to the casualty officer as he left. The slight commotion as an ambulance drew up and a patient was wheeled in caused him to turn his head. He glanced at the patient and then looked again.

'Will you stop for a moment?' he asked, and bent over the stretcher. It was Bertha, all right, with a muddy face and a black eye and hair all over the place.

He straightened up. 'I know this young lady. I'll wait while you take a look.'

'Went after a kid running under a car. Kid's OK but the car wheel caught her. Nasty gash on her left leg.' The ambulanceman added, 'Brave young lady.'

Dr Hay-Smythe bent his great height again. 'Bertha?' His voice was quiet and reassuring. She opened the good eye.

'Oliver.' She smiled widely. 'You oughtn't to be working; it's Sunday.'

He smiled then and signalled to the men to wheel the stretcher away. It struck him that despite the dirt and the black eye nothing could dim the beauty of her one good eye, its warm brown alight with the pleasure of seeing him again.

There wasn't too much damage, the casualty officer told him presently—bruising, some painful grazes, a black eye and the fairly deep gash on one leg. 'It'll need a few stitches, and there's a good deal of grit and dirt in the wound. She'd better have a whiff of anaesthetic so that I can clean it up. Anti-tetanus jab too.'

He looked curiously at his companion; Dr Hay-Smythe was a well-known figure at the hospital, occasionally giving anaesthetics and often visiting the patients in his beds on the medical wards. He was well liked and respected, and rumour had it that he was much in demand socially; this small girl didn't seem quite his type...

Dr Hay-Smythe looked at his watch. 'If you could see to her within the next half-hour I'll give a hand. It'll save calling the anaesthetist out.'

Bertha, getting stiffer with every passing minute and aware of more and more sore places on her person, had her eyes closed. She opened the sound one when she heard his voice.

'You have a cut on your leg, Bertha,' he told

her. 'I'm going to give you a whiff of something while it's seen to, then you will be warded.'

'No, no, I must go back home. Cook might wonder where I am.'

'Only Cook?' he gueried gently.

'Crook's got a half-day and my stepmother and Clare have gone to Henley to lunch with friends. There's no need to bother Cook; her sister's there.'

'Very well, but you are to stay here, Bertha. I'll see that your stepmother knows when she returns. Now, how long ago is it since you had your breakfast?'

'Why ever do you want to know? About eight o'clock.'

'Purely a professional question. No, close your eyes; I'm going to give you an injection in the back of your hand.' He turned away and spoke to someone she couldn't see and presently, eyes obediently shut, she felt a faint prick. 'Count up to ten,' he said, his voice reassuringly casual.

She got as far as five.

When she opened her eyes again she was in bed—a corner bed in a big ward—and the casualty officer and Dr Hay-Smythe were standing at the foot of it.

'Ah, back with us.' He turned away for a moment while two nurses heaved her up the bed, rearranged a cradle over her leg and disappeared again.

He studied her thoughtfully; anywhere else she would have minded being stared at like that, but here in hospital it was different; here he was a doctor and she was just another patient.

'Can I go home soon?' she asked.

It was the last place he wished her to go. She looked very small, engulfed in a hospital gown far too large for her, with her face clean now but pale and the damaged eye the only colour about her. Her hair, its mousy abundance disciplined into a plait, hung over one shoulder.

He said after a moment, 'No, you can't, Bertha. You're in one of my beds and you'll stay here until I discharge you.' He smiled suddenly. 'This is Dr Turner, the casualty officer who stitched you up.' And as another young man joined them he went on, 'And this is the medical officer who will look after you—Dr Greyson. I'll go and see your step-mother this afternoon and she will doubtless arrange to send in whatever you need.'

He offered a hand and she took it and summoned up a smile. 'Thank you for all your trouble. I hope I haven't spoilt your day.'

She closed her eyes, suddenly overcome by sleep.

Dr Hay-Smythe waited until the late afternoon before calling at the Soameses' house—too late for tea and too early for drinks—since he had no wish to linger there. He was admitted by Cook, since Crook was still enjoying his half-day, and ushered into the drawing room, where Mrs Soames and Clare were sitting discussing the lunch party. They greeted him eagerly, bored with each other's company.

'Oliver!' Clare went to meet him. 'How lovely—I was just wondering what I would do with the rest of this dull day, and you're the answer.'

He greeted her mother before replying, 'I'm afraid not. I have to return to the hospital very shortly. I have come to tell you that Bertha has had an accident—'

'The silly girl,' interposed Mrs Soames.

'She saved the life of a small boy who had run into the street in front of a car.' His voice was carefully expressionless. 'She is in hospital with a badly cut leg and severe bruising, so she must stay there for a few days at least. Would you take her whatever is necessary when you go to see her?'

'You've seen her?' Clare's voice was sharp.

'Yes. I happened to be in the accident and emergency department when she was admitted. She is in very good hands. I'll write down the name of the ward for you—there is no reason why you shouldn't visit her this evening.'

'Quite impossible, Oliver. I've guests coming for dinner.' Mrs Soames uttered the lie without

BETTY NEELS                    87

hesitation. 'And I can't allow Clare to go. She is so sensitive to pain and distressing scenes; besides, who knows what foul germs there are in those public wards? She *is* in a public ward?'

'Yes. Perhaps you would ask one of your staff.' He paused, and then went on silkily, 'Better still, if you could give me whatever is needed, I will take it to Bertha.'

This suggestion met with the instant rejection he had expected. 'No, no!' cried Mrs Soames. 'Cook shall go with Bertha's things, and at the same time make sure that she has all she wants. The poor child!' she added with sickening mendacity. 'We must take good care of her when she comes home.'

She gave Clare a warning glance so that the girl quickly added her own sympathy. 'I hope she comes home soon.' Clare sounded wistfully concerned. 'I shall miss her.'

As indeed she would, reflected the doctor. There would be no one to whom she might pass on her unsuitable clothes. She was wearing a ridiculous outfit now, all frills and floating bits; he much preferred Bertha in her startling lime-green. Indeed, upon further reflection he much preferred Bertha, full-stop.

He took his leave presently and went back home to fetch Freddie and take him for a long walk in Hyde Park. And that evening, after he had dined, he got into his car once more and drove to the hospital. Visiting hours were long over and the wards were quiet, the patients drinking their milk or Ovaltine and being settled down for the night. Bertha was asleep when, accompanied by the ward sister, he went to look at her.

'Someone came with her nightclothes and so on?' he wanted to know.

'Oh, yes, Doctor. The family cook—a nice old soul. Gave her a large cake in a tin too, and said she would come again and that if she couldn't come someone called Crook would.'

'Ah, yes, the butler.'

'Has she no family?'

'A stepmother and a stepsister and a father who at present is somewhere in the States. He's a well-known QC.'

Sister looked at him. There was nothing to see on his handsome features, but she sensed damped-down rage. 'I'll take good care of her, Doctor,' she said.

He smiled at her then. 'Good—and will you be sure and let me know before she goes home?'

Bertha, after a refreshing sleep, felt quite herself in the morning. True, she was still stiff and sore, and it was tiresome only having the use of one eye, but she sat up and ate her breakfast and would have got out of bed armed with towel and toothbrush if she hadn't been restrained.

The leg must be rested, she was told. The cut had been deep and very dirty, and until it had been examined and re-dressed she would have to remain in her bed.

There was plenty to keep her interested, however. The elderly lady in the bed next to hers passed half an hour giving her details of her operation, most of them inaccurate, but Bertha listened enthralled until Sister came down the ward with a Cellophaned package.

'These have just come for you, Bertha. Aren't you a lucky girl?'

It was a delicate china bowl filled with a charming mixture of winter crocuses.

'There's a card,' prompted Sister.

Bertha took it from its miniature envelope. The writing on it was hard to read. 'Flowers for Bertha', it said, and then the initials 'O.H-S.'

Sister recognised the scrawl. 'Just the right size for your locker top,' she said breezily, and watched the colour flood into Bertha's pale face. Who'd have thought it? the sister asked herself, sensing romance.

There were visitors later—the small boy whom she had saved led into the ward by his mother and bearing a bunch of flowers. The mother cried all over Bertha and wrung her hand and, very much to Bertha's embarrassment, told everyone near enough to listen how Bertha had saved her small son from being run over.

'Killed, he would have been—or crippled for life. A proper heroine, she is.'

That evening Crook came, bearing more flowers and a large box of chocolates from Cook and the daily and the man who came to do the garden each week.

'Is everything all right at home, Crook?' asked Bertha.

'Yes, Miss Bertha. I understand that there is a letter from your father; he hopes to return within the next few weeks. Mrs Soames and Miss Clare have been down to Brighton with friends; they are dining out this evening.'

'I'm not sure how long I am to stay here, Crook...'

'As long as it takes you to get quite well, Miss Bertha. You're not coming home before.'

He got up to go presently, with the promise that someone would come to see her again.

'Thank you for coming, and please thank the others for the chocolates and flowers. It's so kind of them and I know how busy you all are, so I won't mind if none of you can spare the time to visit. You can see how comfortable I am, and everyone is so friendly.'

On his way out, Sister stopped him. 'You come from Mrs Soames's household? Is she coming to see Miss Soames? She must wish to know about her injuries and I'd like to advise her about her convalescence.'

'Mrs Soames is most unlikely to come, Sister. If you will trust me with any details as to the care of Miss Bertha when she returns home, I shall do my utmost to carry them out,' said Crook.

When Dr Hay-Smythe came onto the ward later that evening, as she was going off duty, Sister paused to talk to him and tell him and the medical officer, who had come to do an evening round, what Crook had told her. 'I'll keep her as long as possible, but I'm always pushed for beds. And although I know you have beds in this ward, doctor, it is a medical unit and Bertha's a surgical case.'

'A couple more days, Sister?' He glanced at the young doctor with him. 'Turn a blind eye, Ralph? At least until the stitches come out. If she goes home too soon she'll be on that leg all day and ruin the CO's painstaking surgery. How is she, by the way?'

'A model patient; she's next to Mrs Jenkins—a thrombosis after surgery—and she's delighted to have such a tolerant listener.' She glanced at the doctor. 'She was delighted with your flowers, doctor.'

'Good. May I see Miss Arkwright for a moment? She wasn't too good yesterday.'

Miss Arkwright was at the other end of the ward

from Bertha, but she could see Dr Hay-Smythe clearly as he went to his patient's bedside. She was feeling sleepy, but she kept her eye open; he would be sure to come and say goodnight presently. Only he didn't. After a few minutes he went away again without so much as a glance in her direction.

Bertha discovered that it was just as easy to cry with one eye as two.

The next few days were pleasant enough—the nurses were friendly, those patients who were allowed up came to sit by her, bringing their newspapers and reading out the more lurid bits, since her eye, now all the colours of the rainbow and beginning to open again, was still painful. Cook came too, this time with a bag of oranges.

Everything was much as usual, she told Bertha comfortably, omitting to mention that Mrs Soames's temper had been worse than usual and that Clare was having sulking fits.

'That nice doctor what she's keen on—always asking 'im ter take 'er out, she is, and 'im with no time to spare. 'E's taking 'er out to dinner this evening, though.'

Bertha stayed awake for a long time that night, listening to the snores and mutterings around her, the occasional urgent cry for a bedpan, the equally urgent whispers for tea. She closed her eyes each time the night nurse or night sister did her round and she heard the night sister say quietly, 'She'll have to go home in a couple of days; she's only here as a favour to Dr Hay-Smythe.'

Bertha lay and thought about going home. She had no choice but to do so for she had no money. It would mean seeing Clare and Oliver together, and she wasn't sure if she could bear that.

I suppose, she reflected, with the clarity of mind which comes to everybody at three o'clock in the morning, that I've been in love with him since he came over to me and asked me if it was my birthday. I'll have to go away... Once Father's back home, perhaps he'll agree to my training for something so that I can be independent. I'll have my own flat and earn enough money to be able to dress well and to go to the hairdresser and have lots of friends... She fell into an uneasy doze.

She was allowed out of bed now, and later the next day Staff Nurse took out alternate stitches. 'I'll have the rest tomorrow,' she said briskly. 'Don't run around too much; it's not quite healed yet. I expect you'll be going home in a day or two now.'

Bertha told Crook that when he came that afternoon. 'Please don't tell anyone, will you? I wouldn't want to upset any plans...'

They both knew Mrs Soames wasn't likely to change any plans she had made just because Bertha was coming home.

Dr Hay-Smythe came to see her that evening. 'You're to go home the day after tomorrow. I'll take you directly after lunch. You feel quite well?'

'Yes, thank you, I'm fine. Some of the stitches are out and it's a very nice scar—a bit red...'

'You won't see it in a few months. Will you be able to rest at home?'

'Oh, of course,' said Bertha airily. 'I can sit in the drawing room. But I don't need to rest, do I? I'm perfectly well. I know my eye's still not quite right, but it looks more dramatic than it is.'

He sat down on the side of the bed. 'Bertha, my mother would like you to go and stay with her for a week or two, perhaps until Christmas. How would you like that?'

Her eyes shone. 'Oh, how kind of her. I'd have to ask my stepmother first...'

He found himself smiling at her eager face. The few days in hospital had done her good; she had a pretty colour and she looked happy. He took her hand in his, conscious of a deep contentment. He had cautioned himself to have patience, to give her time to get to know him, but he had fallen in love with her when he had first seen her and his love had grown over the weeks. She was the girl he had been waiting for, and somehow or other he had managed to keep close to her, despite the dreadful stepmother and the tiresome Clare. He wouldn't hurry her, but after a few days he would go home and tell her that he loved her in the peace and quiet of the country.

He said now, 'We have to talk, Bertha. But not here.'

The ward was very quite and dim. He bent and kissed her gently and went away. Mrs Jenkins, feigning sleep and listening to every word, whispered, 'Now go to sleep, ducks. Nothing like a kiss to give you sweet dreams.'

The next day Oliver realized that he would have to see Mrs Soames before taking Bertha home. There was bound to be unpleasantness and he wanted that dealt with before she arrived. Not that he intended to tell her that he was in love with Bertha and was going to marry her, only that his mother had invited her to stay for a short time.

Mrs Soames gushed over him and then listened to his plans, a smile pinned onto her face. He was surprised at her readiness to agree with him that a week or so's rest was necessary for Bertha, but, thinking about it later, he concluded that it might suit her and Clare to have Bertha out of the way—she would be of no use to them around the house until her leg was quite healed. All the same, he had a feeling of unease.

# CHAPTER FIVE

OLIVER'S feeling of unease was justified. Mrs Soames, left to herself, paced up and down her drawing room, fuming. Bertha had gone behind her back and was doing her best to put a spoke in Clare's wheel. The wretched girl! Something would have to be done.

Mrs Soames, by now in a rage, spent some time thinking of the things she would like to do to Bertha before pulling herself together. Anger wasn't going to help. She must keep a cool head and think of ways and means. She heard Clare's voice in the hall and went to the door and called for her to come to the drawing room.

'Presently,' said Clare, who was halfway up the stairs. 'I've broken a fingernail and I must see to it at once...'

Something in her mother's voice brought her downstairs again.

'What's the matter?'

'Oliver has been here. Bertha is to come home tomorrow and his mother has invited her to stay with her for a couple of weeks.' Mrs Soames almost choked with fury as she spoke. 'The ungrateful girl—going behind our backs. She's cunning enough—she'll have him all to herself if she goes to his home.' She looked thoughtful. 'I wonder— Clare, get me the telephone directory.'

His receptionist was still at his rooms, and, in answer to Mrs Soames's polite enquiry, said that she was afraid that Dr Hay-Smythe wouldn't be seeing new patients during the coming week. 'And he will be going on holiday the following week. But I could book you for an appointment in three weeks' time.'

Mrs Soames put down the phone without bothering to answer.

'He's going on holiday in a week's time—he'll go home, of course, and they'll have a whole week together. We have this week to think of something, Clare.'

Clare poured them each a drink and sat down. 'She'll have to go away—miles away. Now, who do we know…?'

'She'll have to go immediately—supposing he calls to see her?'

'We can say she's spending the weekend with friends.' Clare sat up suddenly. 'Aunt Agatha,' she said triumphantly. 'That awful old crow—Father's elder sister, the one who doesn't like us. We haven't seen her for years. She lives somewhere in the wilds of Cornwall, doesn't she?'

'Perfect—but will she have Bertha to stay? Supposing she refuses?'

'She doesn't need to know. You can send Bertha there—tell her that Aunt Agatha isn't well and has asked if she would go and stay with her.'

'What are we to say? Bertha may want to see the letter…'

'No letter. A phone call.' Clare crowed with laughter. 'I'd love to see her face when Bertha gets there.' She paused to think. 'We'll have to wait until Oliver has brought her home and then pack her off smartly. Do you suppose that he's interested in her? It's ridiculous even to think it. Why, Bertha's plain and dull—it's not possible. Besides, he's taken me out several times…'

'He will again, darling,' said Mrs Soames. She smiled fondly at her daughter; she could rest assured that Clare would get her way.

Bertha was ready and waiting when the doctor came for her. Her leg was still bandaged and her cheek under the black eye was grazed, but all he saw was the radiance of her smile when she saw him. He held down with an iron will a strong desire to gather her into his arms and kiss her, and said merely, 'Quite ready? The leg is comfortable? I can see that the eye is better.'

'I'm fine,' declared Bertha—a prosaic statement,

which concealed her true feelings. 'It's very kind of you to take me home.'

He only smiled, waiting while she said goodbye to Sister and the nurses; she had already visited each bed to shake hands with its occupant.

He carried on a gentle, rambling conversation as he drove her home and as he drew up before the door he said, 'I'm coming in with you, Bertha.' Mrs Soames had seemed pleasant enough, but he still had an uneasy feeling about her.

Mrs Soames and Clare were both there, waiting for them. Clare spoke first.

'Bertha, are you quite better? Ought you to rest?' She gave a small, apologetic smile. 'I'm sorry I didn't come and see you—you know how I hate illness and dreary hospitals. But I'll make it up to you.'

Bertha, recognising this as a deliberate act to put her stepsister in a good light, murmured back and replied suitably to her stepmother's enquiries, which gave Clare the opportunity to take the doctor aside on the pretext of enquiring as to Bertha's fitness.

'Is she all right to walk about? Not too much, of course. We'll take good care of her.' She smiled up into his face. 'It is so kind of your mother to have her to stay. Will you be going to your home too?'

He looked down at her, his face bland. 'I shall

do my best.' He got up from the sofa where they were sitting. 'I must go. I have several patients to see this afternoon.' He crossed the room to where Bertha was in uneasy conversation with her stepmother. 'I will come for you in three days' time, Bertha. Mrs Soames, I'm sure you'll take good care of her until then.' He shook hands then turned to Bertha. 'I hope to get away at half past twelve—will you be ready for me then?'

'Yes—yes, thank you.'

'Don't try and do too much for a few days.'

No one could fault the way in which he spoke to her—a detached kindness, just sufficiently friendly. Only his eyes gleamed under their lids.

Bertha's stepmother, once the doctor had gone, was so anxious to make sure that Bertha had everything she wanted, wasn't tired, wasn't hungry, or didn't wish to lie down on her bed that Bertha was at pains to discover what had brought about this change of heart.

She wasn't the only one. Crook, going back to the kitchen after he had served dinner, put down his tray and said darkly, 'Depend upon it, this won't last—there's madam begging Miss Bertha to have another morsel and is she comfortable in that chair and would she like to go to bed and someone would bring her a warm drink. Poppycock—I wonder what's behind it?'

\*   \*   \*

Apparently nothing; by the end of the second day Bertha's surprise at this cosseting had given way to pleased relief, and Crook had to admit that Mrs Soames seemed to have had a change of heart. 'And not before time,' he observed.

Bertha went to bed early. She had packed her bag with the miserable best of her wardrobe, washed her hair and telephoned the nursery school to tell the matron that she would be coming back after Christmas if they still wanted her. Since her stepmother was showing such a sympathetic face, Bertha had told her that she was no longer reading to an old lady but to a group of children.

'Why didn't you tell me this?' Mrs Soames strove to keep the annoyance out of her voice.

'I didn't think that it was important or that you would be interested.'

Mrs Soames bit her tongue and summoned up a smile. 'Well, it really doesn't matter, Bertha. I'm sure it is very worthwhile work. Oliver arranged it for you, I expect?'

Bertha said that yes, he had, and didn't see the angry look from her stepmother.

Clare, when told of this, burst into tears. 'You see, Mother, how she has been hoodwinking us all this time. Probably seeing him every day. Well, she'll be gone when he comes. Is it all arranged?'

It was still early morning when Bertha was roused by her stepmother. 'Bertha, I've just had a phone call from your aunt Agatha. She's not well and asks for you. I don't think she's desperately ill, just needs someone there other than the servants. She has always been fond of you, hasn't she? She begged me to ask you to go as soon as possible, and I couldn't refuse.'

'I'm going to Mrs Hay-Smythe today, though…'

'Yes, yes, I know. But perhaps you could go to your aunt just for a day or two.'

'Why must I go? Why should she ask for me?'

'She's elderly—and she's always been eccentric.' Mrs Soames, sensing that she was losing the battle, said with sudden inspiration, 'Suppose you go today? I'll phone her doctor and see if he can arrange for someone to stay with your aunt, then you can come straight back. A day's delay at the most. Your father would want you to go.'

'Oliver expects me to be ready—'

'Write him a note and I'll explain. Believe me, Bertha, if Clare could go in your place she would, but you know how your aunt dislikes her.'

Bertha threw back the bed clothes. 'Very well, but I'm coming back, whatever arrangements are made.'

'Well, of course you are. Get dressed quickly and I'll find out about trains.'

Mrs Soames went away to tell Clare that their plan was working so far. 'I told her that I was finding out about the next train.' She glanced at the clock. 'I've just time to dress and drive her to Paddington. She can have breakfast on the train.' She turned at the door. 'Bertha's writing a note for Oliver. Get rid of it before he comes—and not a word to the servants. I'll see them when I get back. I don't mean to tell them where she has gone.'

An hour later, sitting in the train, eating a breakfast she didn't want, Bertha tried to sort out the morning's happenings. It didn't occur to her that she had been tricked; she knew that her stepmother didn't like her, but that she would descend to such trickery never crossed her mind. She had written to Oliver—a careful little note, full of apologies, hoping that he wouldn't be inconvenienced and hoping to see his mother as soon as she could return.

Clare had read it before she'd torn it into little pieces.

The train journey was a lengthy one. Bertha, eating another meal she didn't want, thought about Oliver. He would have been to her home by now, of course, and been told about her sudden departure. She wished she could have written a longer letter, but there hadn't been time. She could think of nothing else, her head full of the whys and wherefores of something she couldn't understand. It was a relief when Truro was reached at last and she got out to change to a local train, which stopped at every station until it stopped, at last, at her destination.

The village was small and she remembered it well from visits when she was a child. Miss Soames lived a mile or two away from the narrow main street, and Bertha was relieved to see a taxi in the station yard. She had been given money for her expenses—just sufficient to get her to her aunt's house—and since her stepmother had pointed out that there was no point in getting a return ticket as she herself would drive down and fetch Bertha she had accepted the situation willingly enough. Her head full of Oliver, nothing else mattered.

Her aunt's house looked exactly the same as she remembered it—solid and rather bleak, with a splendid garden. Bertha toiled up the path with her suitcase and knocked at the door.

After a moment it was flung open and Miss Agatha Soames, majestic in a battered felt hat and old and expensive tweeds, stood surveying Bertha.

'Well, upon my word. Why are you here, gel?'

Bertha, not particularly put out by this welcome, for her aunt was notoriously tart, said composedly that her stepmother had sent her. 'She told me that you were ill and needed a companion and had asked for me urgently.'

Miss Soames breathed deeply. 'It seems to me

from the look of you that it is you who needs a companion. Your stepmother is a vulgar, scheming woman who would be glad to see me dead. I am in the best of health and need no one other than Betsy and Tom. You may return home.' She bent a beady eye on Bertha. 'Why have you a black eye? She actually sent you here to me?'

'Yes, Aunt Agatha.' Awful doubts were crowding into Bertha's tired head.

Miss Soames snorted. 'Then she's up to something. Wants you out of the way in a hurry. Been upsetting the applecart, have you? Poaching on that Clare's preserves, are you?'

When Bertha's cheeks grew pink, she said, 'Took a fancy to you instead of her, did he? Well, if he's got any sense he will come after you.'

Bertha shook her head. 'No, I don't think so. He doesn't know where I am—I didn't tell him.'

'They won't tell him either. But if he's worth his salt he'll find you. Love him?'

'Yes, Aunt Agatha. But he doesn't think of me like that, though he's a kind man.'

'We will see.' Miss Soames thrust the door wide open and said belatedly, 'Well, come in. Now you're here you'd better stay. Where's your father?'

'I'm not exactly sure, but he's coming home soon.'

Aunt Agatha said, 'Pah!' and raised her voice.

'Betsy, come here and listen to this.' Betsy came so quickly that Bertha wondered if she had been standing behind the door.

'No need to tell, I heard it all. Poor lamb. I'll get the garden room ready and a morsel of food. The child looks starved—and look at that eye! A week or two here with good food and fresh air is what she needs.'

During the next few days that was what Bertha got. Moreover, her aunt ordered Tom to bring the elderly Rover to the front door and she and Bertha were driven into Truro, where she sailed in and out of various shops buying clothes for her niece.

When Bertha protested, she said, 'I'll not have a niece of mine wearing cast-off clothes which are several sizes too big and quite unsuitable. I shall speak to your father. Don't interfere, miss.'

So Bertha thanked her aunt and got joyfully into skirts and blouses and dresses which fitted her slender person and were made of fine material in soft colours. If only Oliver could see her now. She had talked to her aunt about what she should do and that lady had said, 'Do nothing, gel. Let your stepmother wonder, if she can be bothered to do so. You are not to write to her nor are you to telephone. You will stay here until this doctor finds you.'

'He won't,' said Bertha. 'He'll never find me...'

'Have you never heard of the proverb "Love
finds a way"? I have great faith in proverbs,' said
Aunt Agatha.

Oliver had presented himself at half past twelve
exactly to collect Bertha, and had been shown into
the drawing room. Mrs Soames had come to meet
him.

'Oliver, thank heaven you have come. I tried to
get you on the phone, but there was no answer.'

She'd found his calm unnerving.

'Bertha!' she'd exclaimed. 'She must be ill—
that accident. She got me out of bed early this
morning and insisted on being driven to Euston
Station. I begged her to stay, to phone you, to wait
at least until you came. She was quite unlike herself—so cold and determined.'

'You did as she asked?' His voice had been very
quiet.

'What else could I do? She wouldn't listen to
reason.'

'She had money? Did she say where she was
going?'

'I gave her what I had. She told me that she was
going to an aunt—a relation of her mother's, I believe, who lives somewhere in Yorkshire. I begged
her to tell why she wanted to leave us and I reminded her that she was to visit your mother—she
said she would write to you.' Mrs Soames man-

aged to squeeze out a tear. 'I really don't know what to do, Oliver. Clare is terribly upset.'

Oliver sounded quite cheerful. 'Why, I suggest that we wait until one or other of us gets a letter. She is quite capable of looking after herself, is she not?'

'Yes, of course. Will you come this evening so that we three can put our heads together? Dinner, perhaps?'

'Not possible, I'm afraid, Mrs Soames.' He spoke pleasantly, longing to wring the woman's neck. There was something not right about the story she had told him. He would get to the bottom of it if it took him weeks, months...

'The whole thing is fishy,' he told Freddie as he drove away. Someone somewhere would know where Bertha had gone; he would send Cully round later with some excuse or other and he could talk to Crook—both he and Cook were obviously fond of Bertha, and in the meanwhile he would see if the nursery school knew anything.

'Gone?' asked Matron. 'Without a word to anyone? I find that hard to believe. Why, she telephoned not a day or two ago to say that she would be coming back after Christmas, when she had had a short holiday.'

Oliver thanked her. It hadn't been much help, but it was a start.

Cully's visit had no success, either. Crook was

disturbed that Bertha had gone so unexpectedly, but he had no idea where she might be. Certainly there was an aunt of hers somewhere in the north of England, and the master had a sister living, but he had no idea where.

The doctor phoned his mother and sat down to think. Mrs Soames had been very glib, and he didn't believe a word of what she had said, but there was no way of getting her to tell the truth. To find this aunt in Yorkshire when he had no idea of her name or where she lived was going to be difficult. Her father's sister—unmarried, Crook had said—was a more likely possibility. He went to bed at last, knowing what he would do in the morning.

Mr Soames QC was well-known in his own profession. The doctor waited patiently until a suitable hour the next morning and then phoned his chambers.

'No,' he was told. 'Mr Soames is still in the States. Would you like to make an appointment at some future date?'

The doctor introduced himself. 'You are his chief clerk? So I can speak freely to you? I am a friend of the Soames family and there is a personal matter I should like to attend to—preferably with Mr Soames. Failing that, has he a relation to whom I could write? This is a family matter, and Mrs Soames is not concerned with it.'

'Dr Hay-Smythe? You have a practice in Harley Street. I remember that you were called to give evidence some time ago.'

'That is so. You would prefer me to come and see you?'

'No. No, that won't be necessary. Mr Soames has a sister living in Cornwall. I could give you her address.' The clerk sounded doubtful.

'I will come to your chambers to collect it, and if you wish to let Mr Soames know of my request, please do so.'

It was impossible to go down to Cornwall for at least two days; he had patients to see, a ward round at the hospital, an outpatients clinic, and then, hours before he intended to leave, an urgent case. So, very nearly a week had passed by the time he got into his car with Freddie and began the long drive down to Cornwall.

It was already later than he had intended; he had no hope of reaching Miss Soames's house at a reasonable hour. He drove steadily westward, Freddie alert beside him, and stopped for the night at Liskeard in an old friendly pub where he was given a hearty supper before going to his room, which was low-ceilinged and comfortable. Since Freddie had behaved in a very well-bred manner he accompanied his master, spreading his length across the foot of the bed.

'This is definitely not allowed,' Oliver told him.
'But just this once, since it is a special occasion. I
only hope that Bertha's aunt likes dogs.'

Freddie yawned.

They were on their way again after breakfast—
bacon, mushrooms freshly picked, fried bread, a
sausage or two and egg garnished with a tomato.
A meal to put heart into a faint-hearted man—
something which the doctor was not. In an hour or
so he would see his Bertha again, beyond that he
didn't intend to think for the moment. He whistled
as he drove and Freddie, no lover of whistling,
curled his lip.

It was shortly after ten o'clock when Betsy carried
the coffee tray into Miss Soames's sitting room,
which was small and pleasant, overlooking the
wide stretch of garden at the back of the house.
Bertha was out there, walking slowly, her hair in
a plait over one shoulder, and wearing one of the
pretty winter dresses which Miss Soames had
bought for her.

Her aunt, peering over her spectacles at her, observed, 'The girl's not pretty, but there's something
about her… Takes after our side of the family, of
course.' She poured her coffee. 'Leave the child
for the moment, Betsy. She's happy.'

Betsy went away, but she was back again within
a minute.

'There's an 'andsome motor car coming up to the door…'

Miss Soames sipped her coffee. 'Ah, yes, I was expecting that. Show the gentleman in here, Betsy, and say nothing to Bertha.'

The doctor came in quietly. 'Miss Soames? I apologise for calling upon you unexpectedly. I believe that Bertha is staying with you?' He held out a hand. 'Oliver Hay-Smythe.'

She took the hand. 'What kept you, young man?' she wanted to know tartly. 'Of course, I knew that you would come, although Bertha is sure that she will never see you again.'

He followed her gaze out of the window; Bertha looked very pretty, and his rather tired face broke into a smile.

'I told her that if a man was worth his salt he would find her even if he had to search the world for her.' She gave him a level gaze. 'Would you do that, Doctor?'

'Yes. I do not quite understand why she is here. I think that her stepmother wanted her out of the way. That doesn't matter for the moment, but it took me some time to discover where she was.'

'You have driven down from London? What have you done with your patients?'

He smiled. 'It took a good deal of organising, but I'd planned a holiday this week.'

'You'll stay here, of course.' She looked over his shoulder. 'What is it, Betsy?'

'There's a dog with his head out of the car window.'

'Freddie. Might I allow him out? He's well-mannered.'

'Get the beast, Betsy,' commanded Miss Soames, and when Freddie, on his best behaviour, came into the room, she offered him a biscuit.

'Well, go along, young man. There's a door into the garden at the back of the hall.'

Freddie, keeping close to his heels, gave a pleased bark as he saw Bertha, and she turned round as he bounded towards her. She knelt and put her arms round his neck and watched Oliver crossing the lawn to her. The smile on her face was like a burst of sunshine as she got slowly to her feet. He saw with delight that she had a pretty colour in her cheeks and a faint plumpness which a week's good food had brought about. Moreover, the dress she was wearing revealed the curves which Clare's misfits had so successfully hidden.

He didn't say anything, but took her in his arms and held her close. Presently he spoke. 'I came as soon as I could, my darling. I had to find you first…'

'How?' asked Bertha. 'Who…?'

'Later, my love.' He bent his head and kissed her.

Bertha, doing her best to be sensible, said, 'But I want to know why my stepmother sent me here—she'll be so angry when she finds out.'

'Leave everything to me, dear heart. You need never see her or Clare again if you don't want to. We'll marry as soon as it can be arranged. Would you like Christmas Eve for a wedding?'

He kissed her again, and eventually, when she had stopped feeling light-headed, she said, 'You haven't asked me—you haven't said—'

'That I love you?' He smiled down at her. 'I love you, darling Bertha. I fell in love with you the moment I clapped eyes on you in that hideous pink dress. Will you marry me and love me a little?'

She reached up to put her arms round his neck. 'Of course I'll marry you, dear Oliver, and I'll love you very much for always. Will you kiss me again? Because I rather like it when you do.'

Aunt Agatha, unashamedly watching them from her chair, took out her handkerchief and blew her nose, and to Betsy, who was peering over her shoulder, she said, 'I must need new glasses, for my eyes keep watering!'

She sounded cross, but she was smiling.

# A CHRISTMAS
# ROMANCE

## BY
## BETTY NEELS

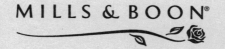

MILLS & BOON®

# CHAPTER ONE

THEODOSIA CHAPMAN, climbing the first of the four flights which led to her bed-sitter—or, as her landlady called it, her studio flat—reviewed her day with a jaundiced eye. Miss Prescott, the senior dietician at St Alwyn's hospital, an acidulated spinster of an uncertain age, had found fault with everyone and everything. As Theodosia, working in a temporary capacity as her personal assistant, had been with her for most of the day, she'd had more than her share of grumbles. And it was only Monday; there was a whole week before Saturday and Sunday...

She reached the narrow landing at the top of the house, unlocked her door and closed it behind her with a sigh of contentment. The room was quite large with a sloping ceiling and a small window opening onto the flat roof of the room below hers. There was a small gas stove in one corner with shelves and a cupboard and a gas fire against the wall opposite the window.

The table and chairs were shabby but there were bright cushions, plants in pots and some pleasant pictures on the walls. There was a divan along the end wall, with a bright cover, and a small bedside table close by with a pretty lamp. Sitting upright in the centre of the divan was a large and handsome ginger cat. He got down as Theodosia went in, trotted to meet her and she picked him up to perch him on her shoulder.

'I've had a beastly day, Gustavus. We must make up for it—we'll have supper early. You go for a breath of air while I open a tin.'

She took him to the window and he slipped out onto the roof to prowl among the tubs and pots she had arranged there. She watched him pottering for a moment. It was dark and cold, only to be expected since it was a mere five weeks to Christmas, but the lamplight was cheerful. As soon as he came in she would close the window and the curtains and light the gas fire.

She took off her coat and hung it on the hook behind the curtain where she kept her clothes and peered at her face in the small square mirror over the chest of drawers. Her reflection stared back at her—not pretty, perhaps, but almost so, for she had large, long-lashed eyes, which were grey and not at all to her taste, but they went well with her ginger hair, which was straight and long and worn in a neat topknot. Her mouth was too large but its corners turned up and her nose was just a nose, although it had a tilt at its tip.

She turned away, a girl of middle height with a

pretty figure and nice legs and a lack of conceit about her person. Moreover, she was possessed of a practical nature which allowed her to accept her rather dull life at least with tolerance, interlarded with a strong desire to change it if she saw the opportunity to do so. And that for the moment didn't seem very likely.

She had no special qualifications; she could type and take shorthand, cope adequately with a word processor and a computer and could be relied upon, but none of these added up to much. Really, it was just as well that Miss Prescott used her for most of the day to run errands, answer the phone and act as go-between for that lady and any member of the medical or nursing staff who dared to query her decisions about a diet.

Once Mrs Taylor returned from sick leave then Theodosia supposed that she would return to the typing pool. She didn't like that very much either but, as she reminded herself with her usual good sense, beggars couldn't be choosers. She managed on her salary although the last few days of the month were always dicey and there was very little chance to save.

Her mother and father had died within a few weeks of each other, victims of flu, several years ago. She had been nineteen, on the point of starting to train as a physiotherapist, but there hadn't been enough money to see her through the training. She had taken a business course and their doctor had heard of a job in the typing pool at St Alwyn's. It had been a lifeline, but unless she could acquire more skills she knew that she had little chance of leaving the job. She would be twenty-five on her next birthday...

She had friends, girls like herself, and from time to time she had been out with one or other of the young doctors, but she encountered them so seldom that friendships died for lack of meetings. She had family, too—two great-aunts, her father's aunts—who lived in a comfortable red-brick cottage at Finchingfield. She spent her Christmases with them, and an occasional weekend, but although they were kind to her she sensed that she interfered with their lives and was only asked to stay from a sense of duty.

She would be going there for Christmas, she had received their invitation that morning, written in the fine spiky writing of their youth.

Gustavus came in then and she shut the window and drew the curtains against the dark outside and set about getting their suppers. That done and eaten, the pair of them curled up in the largest of the two shabby chairs by the gas fire and while Gustavus dozed Theodosia read her library book. The music on the radio was soothing and the room with its pink lampshades looked cosy. She glanced round her.

'At least we have a very nice home,' she told
Gustavus, who twitched a sleepy whisker in reply.

Perhaps Miss Prescott would be in a more cheerful
mood, thought Theodosia, trotting along the wet
pavements to work in the morning. At least she
didn't have to catch a bus; her bed-sitter might not
be fashionable but it was handy...

The hospital loomed large before her, red-brick
with a great many Victorian embellishments. It had
a grand entrance, rows and rows of windows and
a modern section built onto one side where the
Emergency and Casualty departments were
housed.

Miss Prescott had her office on the top floor, a
large room lined with shelves piled high with ref-
erence books, diet sheets and files. She sat at an
important-looking desk, with a computer, two tele-
phones and a large open notebook filled with the
lore of her profession, and she looked as important
as her desk. She was a big woman with commanding features and a formidable bosom—a combi-
nation of attributes which aided her to triumph
over any person daring to have a difference of
opinion with her.

Theodosia had a much smaller desk in a kind of
cubby-hole with its door open so that Miss Prescott
could demand her services at a moment's notice.
Which one must admit were very frequent. Theo-

dosia might not do anything important—like making out diet sheets for several hundreds of people, many of them different—but she did her share, typing endless lists, menus, diet sheets, and rude letters to ward sisters if they complained. In a word, Miss Prescott held the hospital's stomach in the hollow of her hand.

She was at her desk as Theodosia reached her office.

'You're late.'

'Two minutes, Miss Prescott,' said Theodosia cheerfully. 'The lift's not working and I had five flights of stairs to climb.'

'At your age that should be an easy matter. Get the post opened, if you please.' Miss Prescott drew a deep indignant breath which made her corsets creak. 'I am having trouble with the Women's Medical ward sister. She has the impertinence to disagree with the diet I have formulated for that patient with diabetes and kidney failure. I have spoken to her on the telephone and when I have rewritten the diet sheet you will take it down to her. She is to keep to my instructions on it. You may tell her that.'

Theodosia began to open the post, viewing without relish the prospect of being the bearer of unwelcome news. Miss Prescott, she had quickly learned, seldom confronted any of those who had the temerity to disagree with her. Accordingly, some half an hour later she took the diet sheet and began her journey to Women's Medical on the other side of the hospital and two floors down.

Sister was in her office, a tall, slender, good-looking woman in her early thirties. She looked up and smiled as Theodosia knocked.

'Don't tell me, that woman's sent you down with another diet sheet. We had words…!'

'Yes, she mentioned that, Sister. Shall I wait should you want to write a reply?'

'Did she give you a message as well?'

'Well, yes, but I don't think I need to give it to you. I mean, I think she's already said it all…'

Sister laughed. 'Let's see what she says this time…'

She was reading it when the door opened and she glanced up and got to her feet. 'Oh, sir, you're early…'

The man who entered was very large and very tall so that Sister's office became half its size. His hair was a pale brown, greying at the temples, and he was handsome, with heavy-lidded eyes and a high-bridged nose upon which was perched a pair of half glasses. All of which Theodosia noticed with an interested eye. She would have taken a longer look only she caught his eye—blue and rather cold—and looked the other way.

He wished Sister good morning and raised one

eyebrow at Theodosia. 'I'm interrupting something?' he asked pleasantly.

'No, no, sir. Miss Prescott and I are at odds about Mrs Bennett's diet. They sent Theodosia down with the diet sheet she insists is the right one...'

He held out a hand and took the paper from her and read it.

'You do right to query it, Sister. I think that I had better have a word with Miss Prescott. I will do so now and return here in a short while.'

He looked at Theodosia and opened the door. 'Miss—er—Theodosia shall return with me and see fair play.'

She went with him since it was expected of her, though she wasn't sure about the fair play; Miss Prescott usually made mincemeat of anyone disagreeing with her, but she fancied that this man, whoever he was, might not take kindly to such treatment.

Theodosia, skipping along beside him to keep up, glanced up at his impassive face. 'You work here too?' she asked, wanting only to be friendly. 'This is such a big place I hardly ever meet the same person twice, if you see what I mean. I expect you're a doctor—well, a senior doctor, I suppose. I expect you've met Miss Prescott before?'

There were climbing the stairs at a great rate.

'You'll have to slow down,' said Theodosia, 'if you want me to be there at the same time as you.'

He paused to look down at her. 'My apologies, young lady, but I have no time to waste loitering on a staircase.'

Which she considered was a rather unkind remark. She said tartly, 'Well, I haven't any time to waste either.'

They reached Miss Prescott's office in silence and he opened the door for her. Miss Prescott didn't look up.

'You took your time. I shall be glad when Mrs Taylor returns. What had Sister to say this time?'

She looked up then and went slowly red. 'Oh—you need my advice, sir?'

He walked up to her desk, tore the diet sheet he held into several pieces and laid them on the blotter before her. He said quietly, 'Miss Prescott, I have no time to waste with people who go against my orders. The diet is to be exactly as I have asked for. You are a dietician, but you have no powers to overrule the medical staff's requests for a special diet. Be so good as to remember that.'

He went quietly out of the room, leaving Miss Prescott gobbling with silent rage. Theodosia studied her alarmingly puce complexion. 'Shall I make a cup of tea?'

'No—yes. I'm upset. That man...'

'I thought he was rather nice,' said Theodosia, 'and he was very polite.'

Miss Prescott ground her teeth. 'Do you know who he is?'

Theodosia, putting teabags into the teapot, said that no, she didn't.

'Professor Bendinck. He's senior consultant on the medical side, is on the board of governors, has an enormous private practice and is an authority on most medical conditions.'

'Quite a lad!' said Theodosia cheerfully. 'Don't you like him?'

Miss Prescott snorted. 'Like him? Why should I like him? He could get me the sack today if he wanted to.' She snapped her mouth shut; she had said too much already.

'I shouldn't worry,' said Theodosia quietly. She didn't like Miss Prescott, but it was obvious that she had had a nasty shock. 'I'm sure he's not mean enough to do that.'

'You don't know anything about him,' snapped Miss Prescott, and took the proffered cup of tea without saying thank you. Theodosia, pouring herself a cup, reflected that she would rather like to know more about him...

The day was rather worse than Monday had been, and, letting herself into her bed-sitter that evening, she heaved a sigh of relief. A quiet evening with Gustavus for company...

There was another letter from her aunts. She was invited to spend the following weekend with them. They had read in their newspaper that the air in London had become very polluted—a day or two in the country air would be good for her. She was expected for lunch on Saturday. It was more of a command than an invitation and Theodosia, although she didn't particulary want to go, knew that she would, for the aunts were all the family she had now.

The week, which had begun badly, showed no signs of improving; Miss Prescott, taking a jaundiced view of life, made sure that everyone around her should feel the same. As the weekend approached Theodosia wished that she could have spent it quietly getting up late and eating when she felt like it, lolling around with the papers. A weekend with the great-aunts was hardly restful. Gustavus hated it—the indignity of the basket, the tiresome journey by bus and train and then another bus; and, when they did arrive, he was only too aware that he wasn't really welcome, only Theodosia had made it plain that if she spent her weekends with her great-aunts then he must go too...

It was Friday morning when, racing round the hospital collecting diet sheets from the wards, Theodosia ran full tilt into the professor, or rather his waistcoat. He fielded her neatly, collected the shower of diet sheets and handed them back to her.

'So sorry,' said Theodosia. 'Wasn't looking where I was going, was I?'

Her ginger head caught fire from a stray shaft of winter sunshine and the professor admired it silently. She was like a spring morning in the middle of winter, he reflected, and frowned at the nonsensical thought.

'Such a rush,' said Theodosia chattily. 'It's always the same on a Friday.'

The professor adjusted the spectacles on his nose and asked, 'Why is that?'

'Oh, the weekend, you know, patients going home and Sister's weekend, too, on a lot of the wards.'

'Oh, yes, I see.' The professor didn't see at all, but he had a wish to stay talking to this friendly girl who treated him like a human being and not like the important man he was. He asked casually, 'And you, miss...er... Do you also go home for the weekend?'

'Well, not exactly. What I mean is, I do have the weekend off, but I haven't got a home with a family, if that's what you mean. I've got quite a nice bed-sitter.'

'No family?'

'Two great-aunts; they have me for weekends sometimes. I'm going there tomorrow.'

'And where is "there"?' He had a quiet, rather deliberate voice, the kind of voice one felt compelled to answer.

'Finchingfield. That's in Essex.'

'You drive yourself there?'

Theodosia laughed. 'Me? Drive? Though I can ride a bike, I haven't a car. But it's quite easy—bus to the station, train to Braintree and then the local bus. I quite enjoy it, only Gustavus hates it.'

'Gustavus?'

'My cat. He dislikes buses and trains. Well, of course, he would, wouldn't he?'

The professor agreed gravely. He said slowly, 'It so happens that I am going to Braintree tomorrow. I'd be glad to give you and Gustavus a lift.'

'You are? Well, what a coincidence; that would be…' She stopped and blushed vividly. 'I didn't mean to cadge a lift off you. You're very kind to offer but I think I'd better not.'

'I'm quite safe,' said the professor mildly, 'and since you didn't know that I would be going to Braintree in the morning you could hardly be accused of cadging.'

'Well, if you don't mind—I would be grateful…'

'Good.' He smiled then and walked away and she, remembering the rest of the diet sheets, raced off to the men's ward… It was only as she handed over the rest of the diet sheets to Miss Prescott that she remembered that he hadn't asked her where she lived nor had he said at what time he would pick her up. So that's that, reflected Theodosia, scarcely listening to Miss Prescott's cross voice.

If she had hoped for a message from him during the day she was to be disappointed. Five o'clock came and half an hour later—for, of course, Miss Prescott always found something else for her to do just as she was leaving—Theodosia raced through the hospital, intent on getting home, and was brought up short by the head porter hailing her from his lodge in the entrance hall.

'Message for you, miss. You're to be ready by ten o'clock. You'll be fetched from where you live.'

He peered at her over his spectacles. 'That's what Professor Bendinck said.'

Theodosia had slithered to a halt. 'Oh, thank you, Bowden,' she said, and added, 'He's giving me a lift.'

The head porter liked her. She was always cheerful and friendly. 'And very nice too, miss,' he said. 'Better than them trains and buses.'

Theodosia, explaining to Gustavus that they would be travelling in comfort instead of by the public transport he so disliked, wondered what kind of car the professor would have. Something rather staid, suitable for his dignified calling, she supposed. She

packed her overnight bag, washed her hair and polished her shoes. Her winter coat was by no means
new but it had been good when she had bought it
and she consoled herself with the thought that winter coats didn't change their style too much. It
would have to be the green jersey dress...

At ten o'clock the next morning she went down
to the front door with Gustavus in his basket and
her overnight bag over her shoulder. She would
give him ten minutes, she had decided, and if he
didn't turn up she would get a bus to Liverpool
Street Station.

He was on the doorstep, talking to Mrs Towzer,
who had a head crammed with pink plastic curlers
and a feather duster in one hand. When she saw
Theodosia she said, 'There you are, ducks; I was
just telling your gentleman friend here that you
was a good tenant. A real lady—don't leave the
landing lights on all night and leaves the bath
clean...'

Theodosia tried to think of something clever to
say. She would have been grateful if the floor had
opened and swallowed her. She said, 'Good morning, Mrs Towzer—Professor.'

'Professor, are you?' asked the irrepressible Mrs
Towzer. 'Well, I never...'

Theodosia had to admire the way he handled
Mrs Towzer with a grave courtesy which left that
lady preening herself and allowed him to stuff

Theodosia into the car, put her bag in the boot, settle Gustavus on the back seat with a speed which took her breath and then drive off with a wave of the hand to her landlady.

Theodosia said tartly, 'It would have been much better if I had gone to the hospital and met you there.'

He said gently, 'You are ashamed of your land-lady?'

'Heavens, no! She's kind-hearted and good-natured, only there really wasn't any need to tell you about turning off the lights...'

'And cleaning the bath!' To his credit the professor adopted a matter-of-fact manner. 'I believe she was paying you a compliment.'

Theodosia laughed, then said, 'Perhaps you are right. This is a very comfortable car.'

It was a Bentley, dark grey, with its leather upholstery a shade lighter.

'I expect you need a comfortable car,' she went on chattily. 'I mean, you can't have much time to catch buses and things.'

'A car is a necessity for my job. You're warm enough? I thought we might stop for coffee presently. At what time do your great-aunts expect you?'

'If I don't miss the bus at Braintree I'm there in time for lunch. But I'll catch it today; I don't expect it takes long to drive there.'

He was driving north-east out of the city. 'If you will direct me I will take you to Finchingfield; it is only a few miles out of my way.'

She looked at his calm profile uncertainly; without his specs he was really very handsome... 'You're very kind but I'm putting you out.'

'If that were the case I would not have suggested it,' he told her. A remark which she felt had put her in her place. She said meekly, 'Thank you,' and didn't see him smile.

Clear out of the city at last, he drove to Bishop's Stortford and turned off for Great Dunmow, and stopped there for coffee. They had made good time and Theodosia, enjoying his company, wished that their journey were not almost at an end. Finchingfield was only a few miles away and all too soon he stopped in front of the great-aunts' house.

It stood a little way from the centre of the village, in a narrow lane with no other houses nearby; it was a red-brick house, too large to be called a cottage, with a plain face and a narrow brick path leading from the gate to its front door. The professor got out, opened Theodosia's door, collected her bag and Gustavus in his basket and opened the gate and followed her up the path. He put the bag and the basket down. 'I'll call for you at about half past six tomorrow, if that isn't too early for you?'

'You'll drive me back? You're sure it's not disturbing your weekend?'

'Quite sure. I hope you enjoy your visit, Theodosia.'

He went back to the car and got in, and sat waiting until she had banged the door knocker and the door was opened. And then he had gone.

Mrs Trickey, the aunt's daily housekeeper, opened the door. She was a tall, thin woman, middle-aged, with a weather-beaten face, wearing an old-fashioned pinny and a battered hat.

'You're early.' She craned her neck around Theodosia and watched the tail-end of the car disappear down the lane. ''Oo's that, then?'

Mrs Trickey had been looking after the aunts for as long as Theodosia could remember and considered herself one of the household. Theodosia said cheerfully, 'Hello, Mrs Trickey; how nice to see you. I was given a lift by someone from the hospital.'

The housekeeper stood aside to let her enter and then went ahead of her down the narrow, rather dark hall. She opened a door at its end, saying, 'Go on in; your aunts are expecting you.'

The room was quite large, with a big window overlooking the garden at the back of the house. It was lofty-ceilinged, with a rather hideous wallpaper, and the furniture was mostly heavy and dark, mid-Victorian, and there was far too much of it.

Rather surprisingly, here and there, were delicate Regency pieces, very beautiful and quite out of place.

The two old ladies got up from their places as Theodosia went in. They were tall and thin with ramrod backs and white-haired, but there the resemblance ended.

Great-Aunt Jessica was the elder, a once handsome woman with a sweet smile, her hair arranged in what looked like a bird's nest and wearing a high-necked blouse under a cardigan and a skirt which would have been fashionable at the turn of the century. It was of good material and well made and Theodosia couldn't imagine her aunt wearing anything else.

Great-Aunt Mary bore little resemblance to her elder sister; her hair was drawn back from her face into a neat coil on top of her head and although she must have been pretty when she was young her narrow face, with its thin nose and thin mouth, held little warmth.

Theodosia kissed their proffered cheeks, explained that she had been driven from London by an acquaintance at the hospital and would be called for on the following evening, and then enquired about the old ladies' health.

They were well, they told her, and who exactly was this acquaintance?

Theodosia explained a little more, just enough

to satisfy them and nip any idea that Mrs Trickey might have had in the bud. The fact that the professor was a professor helped; her aunts had had a brother, be-whiskered and stern, who had been a professor of something or other and it was obvious that the title conferred respectability onto anyone who possessed it. She was sent away to go to her room and tidy herself and Gustavus was settled in the kitchen in his basket. He didn't like the aunts' house; no one was unkind to him but no one talked to him except Theodosia. Only at night, when everyone was in bed, she crept down and carried him back to spend the night with her.

Lunch was eaten in the dining room, smaller than the drawing room and gloomy by nature of the one small window shrouded in dark red curtains and the massive mahogany sideboard which took up too much space. The old ladies still maintained the style of their youth; the table was covered with a starched white linen cloth, the silver was old and well polished and the meal was served on china which had belonged to their parents. The food didn't live up to the table appointments, however; the aunts didn't cook and Mrs Trickey's culinary skill was limited. Theodosia ate underdone beef, potatoes and cabbage, and Stilton cheese and biscuits, and answered her aunts' questions…

After lunch, sitting in the drawing room between them, she did her best to tell them of her days.

Aunt Jessica's questions were always kind but Aunt Mary sometimes had a sharp tongue. She was fond of them both; they had always been kind although she felt that it was from a sense of duty. At length their questions came to an end and the subject of Christmas was introduced.

'Of course, you will spend it here with us, my dear,' said Great-Aunt Jessica. 'Mrs Trickey will prepare everything for us on Christmas Eve as she usually does and I have ordered the turkey from Mr Greenhorn. We shall make the puddings next week…'

'We are so fortunate,' observed Great-Aunt Mary. 'When one thinks of the many young girls who are forced to spend Christmas alone…' Which Theodosia rightly deduced was a remark intended to remind her how lucky she was to have the festive season in the bosom of her family.

At half past four exactly she helped Mrs Trickey bring in the tea tray and the three of them sat at a small table and ate cake and drank tea from delicate china teacups. After the table had been cleared, they played three-handed whist, with an interval so that they could listen to the news. There was no television; the aunts did not approve of it.

After Mrs Trickey had gone home, Theodosia went into the kitchen and got supper. A cold supper, of course, since the aunts had no wish to cook, and once that was eaten she was told quite kindly

that she should go to bed; she had had a long journey and needed her rest. It was chilly upstairs, and
the bathroom, converted years ago from one of the
bedrooms, was far too large, with a bath in the
middle of the room. The water wasn't quite hot so
she didn't waste time there but jumped into bed,
reminding herself that when she came at Christmas
she must bring her hot-water bottle with her...

She lay awake for a while, listening to the old
ladies going to their beds and thinking about the
professor. What was he doing? she wondered. Did
he live somewhere near Finchingfield? Did he have
a wife and children with whom he would spend
Christmas? She enlarged upon the idea; he would
have a pretty wife, always beautifully dressed, and
two or three charming children. She nodded off as
she added a dog and a couple of cats to his household and woke several hours later with cold feet
and thoughts of Gustavus, lonely in the kitchen.

She crept downstairs and found him sitting on
one of the kitchen chairs, looking resigned. He was
more than willing to return to her room with her
and curl up on the bed. He was better than a hot-
water bottle and she slept again until early morning, just in time to take him back downstairs before
she heard her aunts stirring.

Sunday formed a well-remembered pattern:
breakfast with Mrs Trickey, still in a hat, cooking
scrambled eggs, and then church. The aunts wore

beautifully tailored coats and skirts, made exactly
as they had been for the last fifty years or so, and
felt hats, identical in shape and colour, crowning
their heads. Theodosia was in her winter coat and
wearing the small velvet hat she kept especially for
her visits to Finchingfield.

The church was beautiful and the flowers dec-
orating it scented the chilly air. Although the congregation wasn't large, it sang the hymns tunefully.
And after the service there was the slow progress
to the church porch, greeting neighbours and
friends and finally the rector, and then the walk
back to the house.

Lunch, with the exception of the boiled vegetables, was cold. Mrs Trickey went home after
breakfast on Sundays, and the afternoon was spent
sitting in the drawing room reading the *Sunday
Times* and commenting on the various activities in
the village. Theodosia got the tea and presently
cleared it away and washed the china in the great
stone sink in the scullery, then laid the table for
the aunts' supper. It was cold again so, unasked,
she found a can of soup and put it ready to heat
up.

She filled their hot-water bottles, too, and
popped them into their beds. Neither of them ap-
proved of what they called the soft modern way of
living—indeed, they seemed to enjoy their spartan

way of living—but Theodosia's warm heart wished them to be warm at least.

The professor arrived at exactly half past six and Theodosia, admitting him, asked rather shyly if he would care to meet her aunts, and led the way to the drawing room.

Great-Aunt Jessica greeted him graciously and Great-Aunt Mary less so; there was no beard, though she could find no fault with his beautiful manners. He was offered refreshment, which he declined with the right amount of regret, then he assured the old ladies that he would drive carefully, expressed pleasure at having met them, picked up Gustavus's basket and Theodosia's bag and took his leave, sweeping her effortlessly before him.

The aunts, in total approval of him, accompanied them to the door with the wish, given in Great-Aunt Jessica's rather commanding voice, that he might visit them again. 'You will be most welcome when you come again with Theodosia,' she told him.

Theodosia wished herself anywhere but where she was, sitting beside him in his car again. After a silence which lasted too long she said, 'My aunts are getting old. I did explain that I had accepted a lift from you, that I didn't actually know you, but that you are at the hospital...'

The professor had left the village behind, making for the main road. He said impassively, 'It is only natural that they should wish to know who I am. And who knows? I might have the occasion to come this way again.'

Which somehow made everything all right again. In any case she had discovered it was hard to feel shy or awkward with him. 'Did you enjoy your weekend?' she wanted to know.

'Very much. And you? A couple of quiet days away from the hospital can be just what one needs from time to time.'

Perhaps not quite as quiet as two days with the great-aunts, reflected Theodosia, and felt ashamed for thinking it for they must find her visits tiresome, upsetting their quiet lives.

'Shall we stop for a meal?' asked the professor. 'Unless you're anxious to get back? There is a good place at Great Dunmow. I'll have to go straight to the hospital and won't have time to eat.'

'You don't have to work on a Sunday evening?' asked Theodosia, quite shocked.

'No, no, but I want to check on a patient—Mrs Bennett. It will probably be late by the time I get home.'

'Well, of course we must stop,' said Theodosia. 'You can't go without your meals, especially when you work all hours.' She added honestly, 'I'm quite hungry, too.'

'Splendid. I could hardly eat a steak while you nibbled at a lettuce leaf.'

He stopped in the market place at Great Dunmow and ushered her into the Starr restaurant. It was a pleasing place, warm and very welcoming, and the food was splendid. While the professor ate his steak, Theodosia enjoyed a grilled sole, and they both agreed that the bread and butter pudding which followed was perfection. They lingered over coffee until Theodosia said, 'We really ought to go or you'll never get to bed tonight, not if you are going to see your patient when we get back. It's after nine o'clock...'

The professor ignored the time for he was enjoying himself; Theodosia was good company. She was outspoken, which amused him, and, unlike other girls in his acquaintance, she was content with her lot and happy. And she made him laugh. It was a pity that once they got back to London he would probably not see her again; their paths were unlikely to cross.

The rest of their journey went too swiftly; he listened to Theodosia's cheerful voice giving her opinion on this, that and the other, and reflected that she hadn't once talked about herself. When they reached Mrs Towzer's house, he got out, opened her car door, collected Gustavus in his basket and her bag and followed her up the stairs to her attic. He didn't go in—she hadn't invited him anyway—but she offered a hand and thanked him for her supper and the journey. 'I enjoyed every minute of it,' she assured him, looking up at him with her gentle grey eyes. 'And I do hope you won't be too late going to bed. You need your rest.'

He smiled then, bade her a quiet goodnight, and went away, back down the stairs.

# CHAPTER TWO

MONDAY morning again, and a cold one. Theodosia, going shivering to the bathroom on the floor below, envied Gustavus, curled up cosily on the divan. And there was a cold sleet falling as she went to work. A cheerful girl by nature, Theodosia was hard put to view the day ahead with any equanimity. But there was something to look forward to, she reminded herself; the hospital ball was to be held on Saturday and she was going with several of the clerical staff of the hospital.

She hadn't expected that she would be asked to go with any of the student doctors or the young men who worked in the wages department. She was on good terms with them all but there were any number of pretty girls from whom they could choose partners. All the same, when she had gone to earlier years' balls, she had had partners enough for she danced well.

She would need a new dress; she had worn the only one she had on three successive years. She pondered the problem during the day. She couldn't afford a new dress—that was quite out of the question—but someone had told her that the Oxfam shops in the more fashionable shopping streets quite often yielded treasures…

On Tuesday, she skipped her midday dinner, begged an extra hour of Miss Prescott and took a bus to Oxford Street.

The professor, caught in a traffic jam and inured to delays, passed the time glancing idly around him. There was plenty to catch his eye; shoppers thronged the pavement and the shop windows were brilliantly lighted. It was the sight of a gleaming ginger head of hair which caught his attention. There surely weren't two girls with hair that colour…?

The Oxfam lights were of the no-nonsense variety; the shopper could see what he or she was buying. Theodosia, plucking a dove-grey dress off the rails, took it to the window to inspect it better and he watched her as she examined it carefully—the label, the price tag, the seams… It was a pity that the traffic moved at last and he drove on, aware of an unexpected concern that she should be forced to buy someone else's dress.

Theodosia, happily unaware that she had been seen, took the dress home that evening, tried it on and nipped down to the bathroom where there was a full-length mirror. It would do; she would have to take it in here and there and the neck was too low. She brought out her work basket, found a needle and thread and set to. She was handy with her needle but it took a couple of evenings' work till she was satisfied that it would pass muster.

It wasn't as though she was going with a partner, she reminded herself. There would be a great many people there; no one would notice her. Miss Prescott would be going, of course, but any mention of the ball during working hours was sternly rebuked and when Theodosia had asked her what she would be wearing she'd been told not to be impertinent. Theodosia, who had meant it kindly, felt hurt.

She dressed carefully on Saturday evening. The grey dress, viewed in the bathroom looking-glass by the low-wattage bulb, looked all right. A pity she couldn't have afforded a pair of those strappy sandals. Her slippers were silver kid and out of date but at least they were comfortable. She gave Gustavus his supper, made sure that he was warm and comfortable on the divan, and walked to the hospital wrapped in her winter coat and, since it was drizzling, sheltered under her umbrella.

The hospital courtyard was packed with cars for this was an evening when the hospital Board of Governers and their wives, the local Mayor and his wife and those dignitaries who were in some way connected to St Alwyn's came to grace the occasion. Theodosia slipped in through a side door, found her friends, left her coat with theirs in a small room the cleaners used to store their buckets and brooms and went with them to the Assembly Hall where the ball was already under way.

It looked very festive, with paper chains and a Christmas tree in a corner of the stage where the orchestra was. There were balloons and holly and coloured lights and already there were a great many people dancing. Once there, one by one her friends were claimed and she herself was swept onto the dance floor by one of the technicians from the path lab. She didn't know him well and he was a shocking dancer but it was better than hovering on the fringe of the dancers, looking as though dancing was the last thing one wanted to do.

When the band stopped, one of the students with whom she had passed the time of day occasionally claimed her. It was a slow foxtrot and he had time to tell her about the post-mortem he had attended that morning. She listened carefully, feeling slightly sick, but aware that he was longing to talk about it to someone. There were several encores, so that it was possible for him to relate the very last of the horrid details. When the band stopped finally and he offered to fetch her a drink she accepted thankfully.

She had seen the professor at once, dancing with an elegantly dressed woman, and then again with the sister from Women's Medical and for a third time with the Mayor's wife.

And he had seen her, for there was no mistaking that gingery head of hair. When he had danced with all the ladies he was expected to dance with, he made his way round the dancers until he came upon her, eating an ice in the company of the hospital engineer.

He greeted them both pleasantly, and after a few moments of talk with the engineer swept her onto the dance floor.

'You should ask me first,' said Theodosia.

'You might have refused! Are you enjoying yourself?'

'Yes, thank you.' And she was, for he danced well and they were slow foxtrotting again. The hospital dignitaries wouldn't allow any modern dancing; there was no dignity in prancing around waving arms and flinging oneself about...but foxtrotting with a woman you liked was very satisfying, he reflected.

The professor, his eye trained to see details at a glance, had recognised the grey dress. It was pretty in a demure way but it wasn't her size. He could see the tucks she had taken on the shoulders to make a better fit and the neat seams she had taken in at the waist. It would be a pleasure to take her to a good dress shop and buy her clothes which fitted her person and which were new. He smiled at the absurd thought and asked her with impersonal kindness if she was looking forward to Christmas.

'Oh, yes, and it will be three days this year because of Sunday coming in between.' She sounded more enthusiastic than she felt; three days with the aunts wasn't a very thrilling prospect, but she reminded herself that that was ungrateful. She added, by way of apology for thinking unkindly of them, 'The great-aunts enjoy an old-fashioned Christmas.'

He could make what he liked of that; it conjured up pictures of a lighted Christmas tree, masses of food and lots of presents; with a party on Boxing Day...

She underestimated the professor's good sense; he had a very shrewd idea what her Christmas would be like. He glanced down at the ginger top-knot. It would be a mistake to pity her; she had no need of that. He had never met anyone so content with life and so willing to be happy as she, but he found himself wishing that her Christmas might be different.

He resisted the urge to dance with her for the rest of the evening, handed her back to the engineer and spent the next few moments in cheerful talk before leaving her there.

It was at the end of the evening that he went looking for her amongst the milling crowd making their way out of the hospital. She was on her way out of the entrance when he found her. He touched her arm lightly.

'Come along; the car's close by.'

'There's no need... It's only a short walk... I really don't...' She could have saved her breath; she was propelled gently along away from the crowded forecourt, stuffed tidily into the car and told to fasten her seat belt. It was only as he turned out of the forecourt into the street that she tried again. 'This is quite...'

'You're wasting your breath, Theodosia.' And he had nothing more to say until they reached Mrs Towzer's house. No lights were on, of course, and the rather shabby street looked a bit scary in the dark; walking back on her own wouldn't have been very nice...

He got out, opened her door and took the key she had ready in her hand from her, opened the door silently and switched on the dim light in the hall.

Theodosia held out a hand for the key and whispered, 'Thank you for the lift. Goodnight.' And took off her shoes.

The professor closed the door without a sound, picked up her shoes and trod silently behind her as she went upstairs. She was afraid that he might make a noise but he didn't and she had to confess that it was comforting to have him there. Mrs Towzer, with an eye to economy, had installed landing lights which switched off unless one was nippy between landings.

At her own door he took her key, opened the door and switched on the light, gave her back her key and stood aside for her to pass him.

'Thank you very much,' said Theodosia, still whispering. 'Do be careful going downstairs or you'll be left in the dark, and you will shut the street door?'

The professor assured her in a voice as quiet as her own that he would be careful, and bade her goodnight, pushed her gently into the room and closed the door. Back in his car he wondered why he hadn't kissed her; he had very much wanted to.

As for Theodosia, tumbling into bed presently, hugging a tolerant Gustavus, her sleepy head was full of a jumble of delightful thoughts, all of them concerning the professor.

Going for a brisk walk in Victoria Park the following afternoon, she told herself that he had just happened to be there and that common politeness had forced him to give her a lift back. She went home and had a good tea then went to evensong, to pray there for a happy week ahead!

She wasn't sure if it was an answer to her prayers when she received a letter from Great-Aunt Jessica in the morning. She was asked to go to Fortnum & Mason and purchase the items on the enclosed list. 'And you may bring them down next weekend,' wrote her aunt.

Theodosia studied the list: ham on the bone, Gentleman's Relish, smoked salmon, brandy butter, a Stilton cheese, Bath Oliver biscuits, *marrons glacés*, Earl Grey tea, coffee beans, peaches in brandy… Her week's wages would barely pay for them, not that she could afford to do that. She peered into the envelope in the forlorn hope of finding a cheque or at least a few bank notes but it was empty. She would have to go to the bank and draw out the small amount of money she had so painstakingly saved. If she skipped her midday dinner she would have time to go to the bank. Great-Aunt Jessica would pay her at the weekend and she could put it back into her account.

It wasn't until Wednesday that she had the opportunity to miss her dinner. There was no time to spare, so she hurtled down to the entrance, intent on getting a bus.

The professor, on his way to his car, saw her almost running across the forecourt and cut her off neatly before she could reach the street. She stopped in full flight, unable to get past his massive person.

Theodosia said, 'Hello, Professor,' and then added, 'I can't stop…'

A futile remark with his hand holding her firmly.

'If you're in a hurry, I'll drive you. You can't run to wherever you're going like that.'

'Yes, I can…'

'Where to?'

She had no need to answer his question yet she did. 'The bank and then Fortnum & Mason.'

He turned her round and walked her over to his car. Once inside he said, 'Now tell me why you are in such a hurry to do this.'

He probably used that gentle, compelling voice on his patients, and Theodosia felt compelled once more to answer him. She did so in a rather disjointed manner. 'So, you see, if you don't mind I must catch a bus…'

'I do mind. What exactly do you have to buy?'

She gave him the list. 'You see, everything on it is rather expensive and, of course, Great-Aunt Jessica doesn't bother much about money. She'll pay me at the weekend. That's why I have to go to the bank.'

'That will take up too much time,' said the professor smoothly. 'We will go straight to Fortnum & Mason; I'll pay for these and your aunt can pay me. It just so happens,' he went on in a voice to convince a High Court judge, 'that I am going to Braintree again on Saturday. I'll give you a lift and deliver these things at the same time.'

Theodosia opened her mouth to speak, shut it

again and then said, 'But isn't this your lunch hour?'

'Most fortunately, yes; now, let us get this shopping down.'

'Well, if you think it is all right?'

'Perfectly all right and sensible.'

Once there he ushered her in, handed her list over to a polite young man with the request to have the items packed up and ready within the next half an hour or so, and steered her to the restaurant.

'The food department will see to it all,' he told her. 'So much quicker and in the meantime we can have something to eat.'

Theodosia found her tongue. 'But ought I not to choose everything?'

'No, no. Leave everything to the experts; that's what they are here for. Now, what would you like? We have about half an hour. An omelette with French fries and a salad and a glass of white wine?'

It was a delicious meal and all the more delicious because it was unexpected. Theodosia, still breathless from the speed with which the professor had organised everything, and not sure if she hadn't been reckless in allowing him to take over in such a high-handed manner, decided to enjoy herself. This was a treat, something which seldom came her way.

So she ate her lunch, drank the wine and a cup of coffee and followed him back to the food hall,

to find a box neatly packed and borne out to the
car by the doorman. She was ushered into the car,
too, and told to wait while the professor went back
to pay the bill and tip the doorman .

'How much was it?' asked Theodosia anxiously
as he got in beside her.

'Would it be a good idea,' suggested the professor carefully, 'if I kept this food at my house?
There's not any need to unpack it; everything on
the list is there and I have the receipted bill.'

'But why should you do that? It may be a great
nuisance for you or your wife…'

'I'm not married, and my housekeeper will stow
it safely away until Saturday.'

'Well, if it's really no trouble. And how much
was it?'

'I can't remember exactly, but your aunt must
have a good idea of what the food costs and the
bill seemed very reasonable to me. It's in the boot
with the food or I would let you have it.'

'No, no. I'm sure it's all right. And thank you
very much.'

He was driving back to the hospital, taking short
cuts so that she had still five minutes of her dinner
hour left by the time he stopped in the forecourt.
She spent two of those thanking him in a muddled
speech, smiling at him, full of her delightful lunch
and his kindness and worry that she had taken up
too much of his time.

'A pleasure,' said the professor, resisting a wish to kiss the tip of her nose. He got out of the car and opened her door and suggested that she had better run.

Despite Miss Prescott's sharp tongue and ill temper, the rest of her day was viewed through rose-coloured spectacles by Theodosia. She wasn't sure why she felt happy; of course, it had been marvellous getting her shopping done so easily and having lunch and the prospect of being driven to the aunts' at the weekend, but it was more than that; it was because the professor had been there. And because he wasn't married.

She saw nothing of him for the rest of the week but on Friday evening as she left the hospital there was a message for her. Would she be good enough to be ready at ten o'clock in the morning? She would be fetched as before. This time there was no mistaking the twinkle in the head porter's eye as he told her. Over the years he had passed on many similar messages but never before from the professor.

'We're going to the aunts' again,' Theodosia told Gustavus. 'In that lovely car. You'll like that, won't you?'

She spent a happy evening getting ready for the morning, washing her hair, examining her face anxiously for spots, doing her nails, and putting everything ready for breakfast in the morning. It would never do to keep the professor waiting.

She went down to the front door punctually in the morning to find him already there, leaning against Mrs Towzer's door, listening to that lady's detailed descriptions of her varicose veins with the same quiet attention he would have given any one of his private patients. Mrs Towzer, seeing Theodosia coming downstairs, paused. 'Well, I'll tell you the rest another time,' she suggested. 'You'll want to be on your way, the pair of you.'

She winked and nodded at him and Theodosia went pink as she wished them both a rather flustered good morning, trying not to see the professor's faint smile. But it was impossible to feel put out once she was sitting beside him as he drove off. Indeed she turned and waved to Mrs Towzer, for it seemed wrong to feel so happy while her landlady was left standing at her shabby front door with nothing but rows of similar shabby houses at which to look.

It was a gloomy morning and cold, with a leaden sky.

'Will it snow?' asked Theodosia.

'Probably, but not just yet. You'll be safely at your great-aunts' by then.'

He glanced at her. 'Will you be going to see them again before Christmas?'

'No, this is an unexpected visit so that I could

buy all those things.' In case he was thinking that she was angling for another lift she added, 'I expect you'll be at home for Christmas?'

He agreed pleasantly in a voice which didn't invite more questions so she fell silent. When the silence became rather too long, she began to talk about the weather, that great stand-by of British conversation.

But she couldn't talk about that for ever. She said, 'I won't talk any more; I expect you want to think. You must have a lot on your mind.'

The professor debated with himself whether he should tell her that he had her on his mind, increasingly so with every day that passed. But if he did he would frighten her away. Being friendly was one thing but he sensed that she would fight shy of anything more. He was only too well aware that he was considered by her to be living on a different plane and that their paths would never meet. She was friendly because she was a girl who would be friends with anyone. It was in her nature to be kind and helpful and to like those she met and worked with. Even the redoubtable Miss Prescott.

He said now, 'There is no need to make polite conversation with you, Theodosia; do you not feel the same?'

'Well, yes, I do. I mean, it's nice to be with someone and not have to worry about whether they were wishing you weren't there.'

His rather stern mouth twitched. 'Very well put, Theodosia. Shall we have coffee at Great Dunmow?'

They sat a long while over coffee. The professor showed no signs of hurry. His questions were casual but her answers told him a great deal. She wouldn't admit to loneliness or worry about her future; her answers were cheerful and hopeful. She had no ambitions to be a career girl, only to have a steady job and security.

'You wouldn't wish to marry?'

'Oh, but I would—but not to anyone, you understand,' she assured him earnestly. 'But it would be nice to have a husband and a home; and children.'

'So many young women want a career—to be a lawyer, or a doctor, or a high-powered executive.'

She shook her head. 'Not me; I'm not clever to start with.'

'You don't need to be clever to marry?' He smiled a little.

'Not that sort of clever. But being married isn't just a job, is it? It's a way of life.'

'And I imagine a very pleasant one if one is happily married.'

He glanced at his watch. 'Perhaps we had better get on...'

At the great-aunts' house Mrs Trickey, in the same hat, admitted them and ushered them into the drawing room. Aunt Jessica got up to greet them but Aunt Mary stayed in her chair, declaring in a rather vinegary voice that the cold weather had got into her poor old bones, causing her to be something of an invalid. Theodosia kissed her aunts, sympathised with Aunt Mary and hoped that she wasn't expecting to get free medical treatment from their visitor. She had no chance to say more for the moment since Aunt Jessica was asking Theodosia if she had brought the groceries with her.

The professor greeted the two ladies with just the right amount of polite pleasure, and now he offered to fetch the box of food into the house.

'The kitchen?' he wanted to know.

'No, no. We shall unpack it here; Mrs Trickey can put it all away once that is done. You have the receipted bill, Theodosia?'

'Well, actually, Professor Bendinck has it. He paid for everything. I hadn't enough money.' She could see that that wasn't enough to satisfy the aunts. 'We met going out of the hospital. I was trying to get to the bank to get some money. To save time, because it was my dinner hour, he kindly drove me to Fortnum & Mason and gave them your order and paid for it.'

Aunt Mary looked shocked. 'Really, Theodosia, a young girl should not take any money from a gentleman.'

But Aunt Jessica only smiled. 'Well, dear, we are grateful to Professor Bendinck for his help. I'll write a cheque...'

'Perhaps you would let Theodosia have it? She can let me have it later. I shall be calling for her tomorrow evening.'

Aunt Mary was still frowning. 'I suppose you had spent all your money on clothes—young women nowadays seem to think of nothing else.'

Theodosia would have liked to tell her that it wasn't new clothes, more's the pity. It was cat food, and milk, bread and cheese, tea and the cheaper cuts of meat, and all the other necessities one needed to keep body and soul together. But she didn't say a word.

It was the professor who said blandly, 'I don't imagine that Theodosia has a great deal of money to spare—our hospital salaries are hardly generous.'

He smiled, shook hands and took his leave. At the door to the drawing room he bent his great height and kissed Theodosia's cheek. 'Until tomorrow evening.' His smile included all three ladies as he followed Mrs Trickey to the front door.

Great-Aunt Jessica might not have moved with the times—in her young days gentlemen didn't kiss young ladies with such an air, as though they had a right to do so—but she was romantic at heart and now she smiled. It was Great-Aunt Mary who spoke, her thin voice disapproving.

'I am surprised, Theodosia, that you allow a gentleman to kiss you in that manner. Casual kissing is a regrettable aspect of modern life.'

Theodosia said reasonably, 'Well, I didn't allow him, did I? I'm just as surprised as you are, Aunt Mary, but I can assure you that nowadays a kiss doesn't meant anything—it's a social greeting—or a way of saying goodbye.'

And she had enjoyed it very much.

'Shall I unpack the things you wanted?' she asked, suddenly anxious not to talk about the professor.

It was a task which took some time and successfully diverted the old ladies' attention.

The weekend was like all the others, only there was more talk of Christmas now. 'We shall expect you on Christmas Eve,' said Aunt Jessica. 'Around teatime will suit us very nicely.'

That would suit Theodosia nicely, too. She would have to work in the morning; patients still had diets even at Christmas. There would be a tremendous rush getting the diets organised for the holiday period but with luck she would be able to get a late-afternoon train. She must remember to check the times…

In bed much later that night, with Gustavus curled up beside her, she allowed herself to think about the professor. It was, of course, perfectly all right for him to kiss her, she reassured herself, just as she had reassured her aunts: it was an accepted social greeting. Only it hadn't been necessary for him to do it. He was a very nice man, she thought sleepily, only nice wasn't quite the right word to describe him.

It was very cold in church the next morning and, as usual, lunch was cold—roast beef which was underdone, beetroot and boiled potatoes. The trifle which followed was cold, too, and her offer to make coffee afterwards was rejected by the aunts, who took their accustomed seats in the drawing room, impervious to the chill. Theodosia was glad when it was time for her to get the tea, but two cups of Earl Grey, taken without milk, did little to warm her.

She was relieved when the professor arrived; he spent a short time talking to her aunts and then suggested that they should leave. He hadn't kissed her; she hadn't expected him to, but he did give her a long, thoughtful look before bidding his farewells in the nicest possible manner and sweeping her out to the car.

It must have been the delightful warmth in the car which caused Theodosia to sneeze and then shiver.

'You look like a wet hen,' said the professor,

driving away from the house. 'You've caught a cold.'

She sneezed again. 'I think perhaps I have. The church was cold, but the aunts don't seem to mind the cold. I'll be perfectly all right once I'm back at Mrs Towzer's.' She added, 'I'm sorry; I do hope I won't give it to you.'

'Most unlikely. We won't stop for a meal at Great Dunmow, I'll drive you straight back.'

'Thank you.'

It was the sensible thing to do, she told herself, but at the same time she felt overwhelming disappointment. Hot soup, a sizzling omelette, piping hot coffee—any of these would have been welcome at Great Dunmow. Perhaps, despite his denial, he was anxious not to catch her cold. She muffled a sneeze and tried to blow her nose soundlessly.

By the time they reached the outskirts of London she was feeling wretched; she had the beginnings of a headache, a running nose and icy shivers down her spine. The idea of getting a meal, seeing to Gustavus and crawling down to the bathroom was far from inviting. She sneezed again and he handed her a large, very white handkerchief.

'Oh, dear,' said Theodosia. She heaved a sigh of relief at his quiet, 'We're very nearly there.'

Only he seemed to be driving the wrong way.

'This is the Embankment,' she pointed out. 'You missed the way...'

'No. You are coming home with me. You're going to have a meal and something for that cold, then I'll drive you back.'

'But that's a lot of trouble and there's Gustavus...'

'No trouble, and Gustavus can have his supper with my housekeeper.'

He had turned into a narrow street, very quiet, lined with Regency houses, and stopped before the last one in the terrace.

Theodosia was still trying to think of a good reason for insisting on going back to Mrs Towzer's but she was given no chance to do so. She found herself out of the car and in through the handsome door and borne away by a little stout woman with grey hair and a round, cheerful face who evinced no surprise at her appearance but ushered her into a cloakroom at the back of the narrow hall, tut-tutting sympathetically as she did so.

'That's a nasty cold, miss, but the professor will have something for it and there'll be supper on the table in no time at all.'

So Theodosia washed her face and tidied her hair, feeling better already, and went back into the hall and was ushered through one of the doors there. The room was large and high-ceilinged with a bow window overlooking the street. It was furnished most comfortably, with armchairs drawn up on each side of the bright fire burning in the steel grate, a vast sofa facing it, more smaller chairs, a scattering of lamp tables and a mahogany rent table in the bow window. There were glass-fronted cabinets on either side of the fireplace and a long case clock by the door.

Theodosia was enchanted. 'Oh, what a lovely room,' she said, and smiled with delight at the professor.

'Yes, I think so, too. Come and sit down. A glass of sherry will make you feel easier; you'll feel better when you have had a meal. I'll give you some pills later; take two when you go to bed and two more in the morning. I'll give you enough for several days.'

She drank her sherry and the housekeeper came presently to say that supper was on the table. 'And that nice cat of yours is sitting by the Aga as though he lived here, miss. Had his supper, too.'

Theodosia thanked her and the professor said, 'This is Meg, my housekeeper. She was my nanny a long time ago. Meg, this is Miss Theodosia Chapman; she works at the hospital.'

Meg smiled broadly. 'Well, now, isn't that nice?' And she shook the hand Theodosia offered.

Supper was everything she could have wished for—piping hot soup, an omelette as light as air, creamed potatoes, tiny brussels sprouts and little egg custards in brown china pots for pudding. She ate every morsel and the professor, watching the colour creep back into her cheeks, urged her to have a second cup of coffee and gave her a glass of brandy.

'I don't think I would like it…'

'Probably not. I'm giving it to you as a medicine so toss it off, but not too quickly.'

It made her choke and her eyes water, but it warmed her too, and when she had finished it he said, 'I'm going to take you back now. Go straight to bed and take your pills and I promise you that you will feel better in the morning.'

'You've been very kind; I'm very grateful. And it was a lovely supper…'

She bade Meg goodbye and thanked her, too, and with Gustavus stowed in the back of the car she was driven back to Mrs Towzer's.

The contrast was cruel as she got out of the car: the professor's house, so dignified and elegant, and Mrs Towzer's, so shabby and unwelcoming. But she wasn't a girl to whinge or complain. She had a roof over her head and a job and the added bonus of knowing the professor.

He took the key from her and went up the four flights of stairs, carrying her bag and Gustavus in his basket. Then he opened her door and switched on the light and went to light the gas fire. He put the pills on the table and then said, 'Go straight to

bed, Theodosia.' He sounded like an uncle or a big
brother.

She thanked him again and wished him goodnight and he went to the door. He turned round
and came back to where she was standing, studying
her face in a manner which disconcerted her. She
knew that her nose was red and her eyes puffy; she
must look a sight…

He bent and kissed her then, a gentle kiss on her
mouth and quite unhurried. Then he was gone, the
door shut quietly behind him.

'He'll catch my cold,' said Theodosia. 'Why
ever did he do that? I'll never forgive myself if he
does; I should have stopped him.'

Only she hadn't wanted to. She took Gustavus
out of his basket and gave him his bedtime snack,
put on the kettle for her hot-water bottle and turned
the divan into a bed, doing all these things without
noticing what she was doing.

'I should like him to kiss me again,' said
Theodosia loudly. 'I liked it. I like him—no, I'm
in love with him, aren't I? Which is very silly of
me. I expect it's because I don't see many men
and somehow we seem to come across each other
quite often. I must stop thinking about him and
feeling happy when I see him.'

After which praiseworthy speech she took her
pills and, warmed by Gustavus and the hot-water

bottle, presently went to sleep—but not before she had had a little weep for what might have been if life had allowed her to tread the same path as the professor.

# CHAPTER THREE

THEODOSIA felt better in the morning; she had a cold, but she no longer felt—or looked—like a wet hen. She took the pills she had been given, ate her breakfast, saw to Gustavus and went to work. Miss Prescott greeted her sourly, expressed the hope that she would take care not to pass her cold on to her and gave her enough work to keep her busy for the rest of the day. Which suited Theodosia very well for she had no time to think about the professor. Something, she told herself sternly, she must stop doing at once—which didn't prevent her from hoping that she might see him as she went around the hospital. But she didn't, nor was his car in the forecourt when she went home later that day.

He must have gone away; she had heard that he was frequently asked to other hospitals for consultations, and there was no reason why he should have told her. It was during the following morning, on her rounds, that she overhead the ward sister remark to her staff nurse that he would be back for his rounds at the end of the week. It seemed that he was in Austria.

Theodosia dropped her diet sheets deliberately

and took a long time picking them up so that she
could hear more.

'In Vienna,' said Sister, 'and probably Rome.
Let's hope he gets back before Christmas.'

A wish Theodosia heartily endorsed; the idea of
him spending Christmas anywhere but at his lovely
home filled her with unease.

She was quite herself by the end of the week;
happy to be free from Miss Prescott's iron hand,
she did her shopping on Saturday and, since the
weather was fine and cold, decided to go to Sunday's early-morning service and then go for a walk
in one of the parks.

It was still not quite light when she left the
house the next morning and there was a sparkle of
frost on the walls and rooftops. The church was
warm, though, and fragrant with the scent of chry-
santhemums. There wasn't a large congregation
and the simple service was soon over. She started
to walk back, sorry to find that the early-morning
sky was clouding over.

The streets were empty save for the occasional
car and an old lady some way ahead of her.
Theodosia, with ten minutes' brisk walk before
her, walked faster, spurred on by the thought of
breakfast.

She was still some way from the old lady when
a car passed her, going much too fast and swerving
from side to side of the street. The old lady hadn't

a chance; the car mounted the kerb as it reached her, knocked her down and drove on.

Theodosia ran. There was no one about, the houses on either side of the street had their curtains tightly pulled over the windows, and the street was empty; she wanted to scream but she needed her breath.

The old lady lay half on the road, half on the pavement. She looked as though someone had picked her up and tossed her down and left her in a crumpled heap. One leg was crumpled up under her and although her skirt covered it Theodosia could see that there was blood oozing from under the cloth. She was conscious, though, turning faded blue eyes on her, full of bewilderment.

Theodosia whipped off her coat, tucked it gently under the elderly head and asked gently, 'Are you in pain? Don't move; I'm going to get help.'

'Can't feel nothing, dearie—a bit dizzy, like.'

There was a lot more blood now. Theodosia lifted the skirt gently and looked at the awful mess under it. She got to her feet, filling her lungs ready to bellow for help and at the same time starting towards the nearest door.

The professor, driving himself back from Heathrow after his flight from Rome, had decided to go first to the hospital, check his patients there and then go home for the rest of the day. He didn't hurry. It was pleasant to be back in England and London—even the shabbier streets of London— was quiet and empty. His peaceful thoughts were rudely shattered at the sight of Theodosia racing across the street, waving her arms like a maniac.

He stopped the car smoothly, swearing softly, something he seldom did, but he had been severely shaken…

'Oh, do hurry, she's bleeding badly,' said Theodosia. 'I was just going to shout for help for I'm so glad it's you…'

He said nothing; there would be time for words later. He got out of the car and crossed the street and bent over the old lady.

'Get my bag from the back of the car.' He had lifted the sodden skirt. When she had done that he said, 'There's a phone in the car. Get an ambulance. Say that it is urgent.'

She did as she was told and went back to find him on his haunches, a hand rummaging in his bag, while he applied pressure with his other hand to the severed artery.

'Find a forceps,' he told her. 'One with teeth.'

She did that too and held a second pair ready, trying not to look at the awful mess. 'Now put the bag where I can reach it and go and talk to her.' He didn't look up. 'You got the ambulance?'

'Yes, I told them where to come and that it was very urgent.'

She went and knelt by the old lady, who was still conscious but very pale.

'Bit of bad luck,' she said in a whisper. 'I was going to me daughter for Christmas...'

'Well, you will be well again by then,' said Theodosia. 'The doctor's here now and you're going to hospital in a few minutes.'

'Proper Christmas dinner, we was going ter 'ave. Turkey and the trimmings—I like a bit of turkey...'

'Oh, yes, so do I,' said Theodosia, her ears stretched for the ambulance. 'Cranberry sauce with it...'

'And a nice bit of stuffing.' The old lady's voice was very weak. 'And plenty of gravy. Sprouts and pertaters and a good bread sauce. Plenty of onion with it.'

'Your daughter makes her own puddings?' asked Theodosia, and thought what a strange conversation this was—like a nightmare only she was already awake.

'Is there something wrong with me leg?' The blue eyes looked anxious.

'You've cut it a bit; the doctor's seeing to it. Wasn't it lucky that he was passing?'

'Don't 'ave much ter say for 'imself, does 'e?'

'Well, he is busy putting a bandage on. Do you live near here?'

'Just round the corner—Holne Road, number

six. Just popped out ter get the paper.' The elderly face crumpled. 'I don't feel all that good.'

'You'll be as bright as a button in no time,' said Theodosia, and heard the ambulance at last.

Things moved fast then. The old lady, drowsy with morphia now, was connected up to oxygen and plasma while the professor tied off the torn arteries, checked her heart and with the paramedics stowed her in the ambulance.

Theodosia, making herself small against someone's gate, watched the curious faces at windows and doors and wondered if she should go.

'Get into the car; I'll drop you off. I'm going to the hospital.'

He stared down at her unhappy face. 'Hello,' he said gently, and he smiled.

He had nothing more to say and Theodosia was feeling sick. He stopped at Mrs Towzer's just long enough for her to get out and drove off quickly. She climbed the stairs and, once in her room, took off her dirty, blood-stained clothes and washed and dressed again, all the while telling Gustavus what had happened.

She supposed that she should have breakfast although she didn't really want it. She fed Gustavus and put on the kettle. A cup of tea would do.

When there was a knock on the door she called, 'Come in,' remembering too late that she shouldn't have done that before asking who was there.

The professor walked in. 'You should never open the door without checking,' he said. He turned off the gas under the kettle and the gas fire and then stowed Gustavus in his basket.

'What are you doing?' Theodosia wanted to know.

'Taking you back for breakfast—you and Gustavus. Get a coat—something warm.'

'My coat is a bit—that is, I shall have to take it to the cleaners. I've got a mac.' She should have been annoyed with him, walking in like that, but somehow she couldn't be bothered. Besides, he was badly in need of the dry cleaners, too. 'Is the old lady all right?'

'She is in theatre now, and hopefully she will recover. Now, hurry up, dear girl.'

She could refuse politely but Gustavus was already in his basket and breakfast would be very welcome. She got into her mac, pulled a woolly cap over her bright hair and accompanied him downstairs. There was no one about and the street was quiet; she got into the car when he opened the door for her, mulling over all the things she should have said if only she had had her wits about her.

As soon as they had had their breakfast she would tell him that she was having lunch with friends... She discarded the idea. To tell him fibs, even small, harmless ones, was something she found quite impossible. She supposed that was because she loved him. People who loved each other didn't have secrets. Only he didn't love her.

She glanced sideways at him. 'You've spoilt your suit.'

'And you your coat. I'm only thankful that it was you who were there. You've a sensible head under that bright hair; most people lose their wits at an accident. You were out early?'

'I'd been to church. I planned to go for a long walk. I often do on a Sunday.'

'Very sensible—especially after being cooped up in the hospital all week.'

Meg came to meet them as they went into the house. She took Theodosia's mac and cap and said firmly, 'Breakfast will be ready just as soon as you've got into some other clothes, sir. Miss Chapman can have a nice warm by the fire.'

She bustled Theodosia down the hall and into a small, cosy sitting room where there was a bright fire burning. Its window overlooked a narrow garden at the back and the round table by it was set for breakfast.

'Now just you sit quiet for a bit,' said Meg. 'I'll get Gustavus.'

The cat, freed from his basket, settled down before the fire as though he had lived there all his life.

The professor came presently in corduroys and a polo-necked sweater. Cashmere, decided

Theodosia. Perhaps if she could save enough
money she would buy one instead of spending a
week next summer at a bed and breakfast farm.

Meg followed him in with a tray of covered
dishes; Theodosia's breakfasts of cornflakes, toast
and, sometimes, a boiled egg paled to oblivion beside this splendid array of bacon, eggs, tomatoes,
mushrooms and kidneys.

He piled her plate. 'We must have a good breakfast if we are to go walking, too,' he observed.

She stared at him across the table. 'But it is me
who is going walking...'

'You don't mind if I come, too? Besides, I need
your help. I'm going to Worthing to collect a dog;
he'll need a good walk before we bring him back.'

'A dog?' said Theodosia. 'Why is he at
Worthing? And you don't really need me with
you.'

He didn't answer at once. He said easily, 'He's
a golden Labrador, three years old. He belongs to
a friend of mine who has gone to Australia. He's
been in a dog's home for a week or so until I was
free to take him over.'

'He must be unhappy. But not any more once
he's living with you. If you think it would help to
make him feel more at home if I were there, too,
I'd like to go with you.' She frowned. 'I forgot, I
can't. Gustavus...'

'He will be quite happy with Meg, who dotes

on him.' He passed her the toast. 'So that's settled. It's a splendid day to be out of doors.'

They had left London behind them and were nearing Dorking when he said, 'Do you know this part of the country? We'll leave the main road and go through Billingshurst. We can get back onto the main road just north of Worthing.'

Even in the depths of winter, the country was beautiful, still sparkling from the night frost and the sun shining from a cold blue sky. Theodosia, snug in the warmth and comfort of the car, was in seventh heaven. She couldn't expect anything as delightful as this unexpected day out to happen again, of course. It had been a kindly quirk of fate which had caused them to meet again.

She said suddenly, 'That old lady—it seems so unfair that she should be hurt and in hospital while we're having this glorious ride—' She stopped then and added awkwardly, 'What I mean is, I'm having a glorious ride.'

The professor thought of several answers he would have liked to make to that. Instead he said casually, 'It's a perfect day, isn't it? I'm enjoying it, too. Shall we stop for a cup of coffee in Billingshurst?'

When they reached Worthing, he took her to one of the splendid hotels on the seafront where, the shabby raincoat hidden out of sight in the cloakroom, she enjoyed a splendid lunch with him, unconscious of the glances of the other people there, who were intrigued by the vivid ginger of her hair.

It was early afternoon when they reached the dog's home. He was ready and waiting for them, for he recognized the professor as a friend of his master and greeted him with a dignified bark or two and a good deal of tail-wagging. He was in a pen with a small dog of such mixed parentage that it was impossible to tell exactly what he might be. He had a foxy face and bushy eyebrows, a rough coat, very short legs and a long thin tail. He sat and watched while George the Labrador was handed over and Theodosia said, 'That little dog, he looks so sad…'

The attendant laughed. 'He's been George's shadow ever since he came; can't bear to be parted from him. They eat and sleep together, too. Let's hope someone wants him. I doubt it—he came in off a rubbish dump.'

The professor was looking at Theodosia; he knew with resigned amusement that he was about to become the owner of the little dog. She wasn't going to ask, but the expression on her face was eloquent.

'Then perhaps we might have the little dog as well since they are such friends. Has he a name?'

He was rewarded by the happiness in her face. 'He may come, too?' She held out her arms for the little beast, who was shivering with excitement, and he stayed there until the professor had dealt with their payment, chosen a collar and lead for him and they had left the home.

'A brisk walk on the beach will do us all good,' said the professor. 'We must have a name,' he observed as the two dogs ran to and fro. They had got into the car without fuss and now they were savouring their freedom.

'Max,' said Theodosia promptly. 'He's such a little dog and I don't suppose he'll grow much more so he needs an important name. Maximilian—only perhaps you could call him Max?'

'I don't see why not,' agreed the professor. He turned her round and started to walk back to the car. He whistled to the dogs. 'George, Max...'

They came running and scrambled into the car looking anxious.

'It's all right, you're going home,' said Theodosia, 'and everyone will love you.' She remembered then. 'Gustavus—he's not used to dogs; he never sees them...'

'Then it will be a splendid opportunity for him to do so. We will put the three of them in the garden together.'

'We will? No, no, there's no need. If you'll give me time to pop him into his basket, I can take him with me.'

The professor was driving out of Worthing, this time taking the main road to Horsham and Dorking. The winter afternoon was already fading into dusk and Theodosia reflected on how quickly the hours flew by when one was happy.

He hadn't answered her; presumably he had agreed with her. There would be buses, but she would have to change during the journey back to her bed-sitter. She reminded herself that on a Sunday evening with little traffic and the buses half empty she should have an easy journey.

They talked from time to time and every now and then she turned round to make sure the dogs were all right. They were sitting upright, close together, looking uncertain.

'Did you have a dog when you were a little girl?' asked the professor.

'Oh, yes, and a cat. I had a pony, too.'

'Your home was in the country?' he asked casually.

She told him about the nice old house in Wiltshire and the school she had gone to and how happy she had been, and then said suddenly, 'I'm sorry, I must be boring you. It's just that I don't get the chance to talk about it very often. Of course, I think about it whenever I like.' She glanced out of the window into the dark evening. 'Are we nearly there?'

'Yes, and you have no need to apologize; I have

not been bored. I have wondered about your home before you came to London, for you are so obviously a square peg in a round hole.'

'Oh? Am I? I suppose I am, but I'm really very lucky. I mean, I have the great-aunts and a job and I know lots of people at the hospital.'

'But perhaps you would like to do some other work?'

'Well, I don't think I'm the right person to have a career, if you mean the sort who wear those severe suits and carry briefcases...'

He laughed then, but all he said was, 'We're almost home.'

If only it were home—her home, thought Theodosia, and then told herself not to be a silly fool. She got out when he opened her door and waited while he took up the dogs' leads and ushered them to the door. When she hesitated he said, 'Come along, Theodosia. Meg will have tea waiting for us.'

Much later, lying in bed with Gustavus curled up beside her, Theodosia thought over her day, minute by minute. It had been like a lovely dream, only dreams were forgotten and she would never forget the hours she had spent with the professor. And the day had ended just as he had planned it beforehand; they had had tea by the fire with the two dogs sitting between them as though they had lived

there all their lives. Although she had been a bit
scared when the professor had fetched Gustavus
and introduced him to the dogs, she had said nothing. After a good deal of spitting and gentle growl-
ing the three animals had settled down together.

She had said that she must go back after tea, but
somehow he'd convinced her that it would be far
better if she stayed for supper. 'So that Gustavus
can get used to George and Max,' he had explained
smoothly. She hated leaving his house and her bed-
sitter was cold and uninviting.

The professor had lighted the gas fire for her,
drawn the curtains over the window and turned on
the table lamp, before going to the door, smiling
at her muddled thanks and wishing her goodnight
in a brisk manner.

There was no reason why he should have lingered, she told herself sleepily. Perhaps she would
see him at the hospital—not to talk to, just to get
a glimpse of him would do, so that she knew that
he was still there.

In the morning, when she woke, she told herself
that any foolish ideas about him must be squashed.
She couldn't pretend that she wasn't in love with
him, because she was and there was nothing she
could do about that, but at least she would be sensible about it.

This was made easy for her since Miss Prescott
was in a bad mood. Theodosia had no time at all

to think about anything but the endless jobs her superior found for her to do, but in her dinner hour she went along to the women's surgical ward and asked if she might see the old lady.

She was sitting propped up in bed, looking surprisingly cheerful. True, she was attached to a number of tubes and she looked pale, but she remembered Theodosia at once.

'I'd have been dead if you hadn't come along, you and that nice doctor. Patched me up a treat, they have! My daughter's been to see me, too. Ever so grateful, we both are.'

'I'm glad I just happened to be there, and it was marvellous luck that Professor Bendinck should drive past...'

'Professor, is he? A very nice gentleman and ever so friendly. Came to see me this morning.'

Just to know that he had been there that morning made Theodosia feel happy. Perhaps she would see him too...

But there was no sign of him. The week slid slowly by with not so much as a glimpse of him. Friday came at last. She bade Miss Prescott a temporary and thankful goodbye and made her way through the hospital. It had been raining all day and it was cold as well. A quiet weekend, she promised herself, making for the entrance.

The professor was standing by the main door and she saw him too late to make for the side door.

As she reached him she gave him a cool nod and was brought to a halt by his hand.

'There you are. I was afraid that I had missed you.'

'I've been here all this week,' said Theodosia, aware of the hand and filled with delight, yet at the same time peevish.

'Yes, so have I. I have a request to make. Would you be free on Sunday to take the dogs into the country? George is very biddable, but Max needs a personal attendant.' He added, most unfairly, 'And since you took such an interest in him...'

She felt guilty. 'Oh, dear. I should have thought... It was my fault, wasn't it? If I hadn't said anything... Ought he to go back to Worthing and find another owner?'

'Certainly not. It is merely a question of him settling down. He is so pleased to be with George that he gets carried away. They couldn't be separated.' He had walked her through the door. 'I'll drive you home...'

'There's no need.'

Which was a silly remark for it was pouring with rain, as well as dark and cold.

She allowed herself to be stowed in the car and when they got to Mrs Towzer's house he got out with her. 'I'll be here at ten o'clock on Sunday,' he told her, and didn't wait for her answer.

'Really,' said Theodosia, climbing the stairs. 'He does take me for granted.'

But she knew that wasn't true. He merely arranged circumstances in such a way that he compelled her to agree to what he suggested.

She was up early on Sunday morning, getting breakfast for herself and Gustavus, explaining to him that she would have to leave him alone. 'But you shall have something nice for supper,' she promised him. The professor hadn't said how long they would be gone, or where. She frowned. He really did take her for granted; next time she would have a good excuse...

It was just before ten o'clock when he knocked on her door. He wished her good morning in a casual manner which gave her the feeling that they had known each other all their lives. 'We'll take Gustavus, if you like. He'll be happier in the car than sitting by himself all day.'

'Well, yes, perhaps—if George and Max won't mind and it's not too long.'

'No distance.' He was settling Gustavus in his basket. 'A breath of country air will do him good.'

Mrs Towzer wasn't in the hall but her door was just a little open. As the professor opened the door he said, 'We shall be back this evening, Mrs Towzer,' just as her face appeared in the crack in the door.

'She's not being nosy,' said Theodosia as they drove away. 'She's just interested.'

She turned her head a little and found George and Max leaning against her seat, anxious to greet her and not in the least bothered by Gustavus in his basket. She was filled with happiness; it was a bright, cold morning and the winter sun shone, the car was warm and comfortable and she was sitting beside the man she loved. What more could a girl want? A great deal, of course, but Theodosia, being the girl she was, was content with what she had at the moment.

'Where are we going?' she asked presently. 'This is the way to Finchingfield.'

'Don't worry, we are not going to your great-aunts'. I have a little cottage a few miles from Saffron Walden; I thought we could go there, walk the dogs and have a picnic lunch. Meg has put something in a basket for us.'

He didn't take the motorway but turned off at Brentwood and took the secondary roads to Bishop's Stortford and after a few miles turned off again into a country road which led presently to a village. It was a small village, its narrow main street lined with small cottages before broadening into a village green ringed by larger cottages and several houses, all of them overshadowed by the church.

The professor turned into a narrow lane leading

from the green and stopped, got out to open a gate in the hedge and then drove through it along a short paved driveway, with a hedge on one side of it and a fair-sized garden on the other, surrounding a reed-thatched, beetle-browed cottage with a porch and small latticed windows, its brick walls faded to a dusty pink. The same bricks had been used for the walls on either side of it which separated the front garden from the back of the house, pierced by small wooden doors.

The professor got out, opened Theodosia's door and then released the dogs.

'Gustavus…' began Theodosia.

'We will take him straight through to the garden at the back. There's a high wall, so he'll be quite safe there and he can get into the cottage.'

He unlocked one of the small doors and urged her through with the dogs weaving themselves to and fro and she could see that it was indeed so; the garden was large, sloping down to the fields and surrounded by a high brick wall. It was an old-fashioned garden with narrow brick paths between beds which were empty now, but she had no doubt they would be filled with rows of orderly vegetables later on. Beyond the beds was a lawn with fruit bushes to one side of it and apple trees.

'Oh, how lovely—even in winter it's perfect.'

He sat Gustavus's basket down, opened it and

presently Gustavus poked out a cautious head and then sidled out.

'He's not used to being out of doors,' said Theodosia anxiously, 'only on the roof outside my window. At least, not since I've had him. He was living on the streets before that, but that's not the same as being free.'

She had bent to stroke the furry head and the professor said gently, 'Shall we leave him to get used to everything? The dogs won't hurt him and we can leave the kitchen door open.'

He unlocked the door behind him and stood aside for her to go inside. The kitchen was small, with a quarry-tiled floor, pale yellow walls and an old-fashioned dresser along one wall. There was an Aga, a stout wooden table and equally stout chairs and a deep stone sink. She revolved slowly, liking what she saw; she had no doubt that the kitchen lacked nothing a housewife would need, but it was a place to sit cosily over a cup of coffee, or to come down to in the morning and drink a cup of tea by the open door...

'Through here,' said the professor, and opened a door into the hall.

It was narrow, with a polished wooden floor and cream-painted walls. There were three doors and he opened the first one. The living room took up the whole of one side of the cottage, with little windows overlooking the front garden and French

windows opening onto the garden at the back. It
was a delightful room with easy chairs, tables here
and there and a wide inglenook. The floor was
wooden here, too, but there were rugs on it, their
faded colours echoing the dull reds and blues of
the curtains. There were pictures on the walls but
she was given no chance to look at them.

'The dining room,' said the professor as she
crossed the hall. It was a small room, simply furnished with a round table, chairs and a sideboard,
and all of them, she noted, genuine pieces in dark
oak.

'And this is my study.' She glimpsed a small
room with a desk and chair and rows of bookshelves.

The stairs were small and narrow and led to a
square landing. There were three bedrooms, one
quite large and the others adequate, and a bathroom. The cottage might be old but no expense
had been spared here. She looked at the shelves
piled with towels and all the toiletries any woman
could wish for.

'Fit for a queen,' said Theodosia.

'Or a wife...'

Which brought her down to earth again. 'Oh, are
you thinking of getting married?'

'Indeed, I am.'

She swallowed down the unhappiness which

was so painful that it was like a physical hurt. 'Has she seen this cottage? She must love it...'

'Yes, she has seen it and I think that she has found it very much to her taste.'

She must keep on talking. 'But you won't live here? You have your house in London.'

'We shall come here whenever we can.'

'The garden is lovely. I don't suppose you have much time to work in it yourself.'

'I make time and I have a splendid old man who comes regularly, as well as Mrs Trump who comes every day when I'm here and keeps an eye on the place when I'm not.'

'How nice,' said Theodosia inanely. 'Should I go and see if Gustavus is all right?'

He was sitting by his basket looking very composed, ignoring the two dogs who were cavorting around the garden.

'It's as though he's been here all his life,' said Theodosia. She looked at the professor. 'It's that kind of house, isn't it? Happy people have lived in it.'

'And will continue to do so. Wait here; I'll fetch the food.'

They sat at the kitchen table eating their lunch; there was soup in a Thermos; little crusty rolls filled with cream cheese and ham, miniature sausage rolls, tiny buttery croissants and piping hot coffee from another Thermos. There was food for the animals as well as a bottle of wine. Theodosia ate with the pleasure of a child, keeping up a rather feverish conversation. She was intent on being cool and casual, taking care to talk about safe subjects—the weather, Christmas, the lighter side of her work at the hospital. The professor made no effort to change the subject, listening with tender amusement to her efforts and wondering if this would be the right moment to tell her that he loved her. He decided it was not, but he hoped that she might begin to do more than like him. She was young; she might meet a younger man. A man of no conceit, he supposed that she thought of him as a man well past his first youth.

They went round the garden after lunch with Gustavus in Theodosia's arms, the dogs racing to and fro, and when the first signs of dusk showed they locked up the little house, stowed the animals in the car and began the drive back to London.

They had reached the outskirts when the professor's bleeper disturbed the comfortable silence. Whoever it was had a lot to say but at length he said, 'I'll be with you in half an hour.' Then he told Theodosia, 'I'll have to go to the hospital. I'll drop you off on the way. I'm sorry; I had hoped that you would have stayed for supper.'

'Thank you, but I think I would have refused; I have to get ready for work tomorrow—washing and ironing and so on.' She added vaguely, 'But it's kind of you to invite me. Thank you for a lovely day; we've enjoyed every minute of it!' Which wasn't quite true, for there had been no joy for her when he'd said that he was going to get married.

When they reached Mrs Towzer's she said, 'Don't get out; you mustn't waste a moment…'

He got out all the same without saying anything, opened the door for her, put Gustavus's basket in the hall and then drove away with a quick nod.

'And that is how it will be from now on,' muttered Theodosia, climbing the stairs and letting herself into her cold bed-sitter. 'He's not likely to ask me out again, but if he does I'll not go. I must let him see that we have nothing in common; it was just chance meetings and those have to stop!'

She got her supper—baked beans on toast and a pot of tea—fed a contented Gustavus and presently went to bed to cry in comfort until at last she fell asleep.

# CHAPTER FOUR

THE week began badly. Theodosia overslept;
Gustavus, usually so obedient, refused to come in
from the roof; and the coil of ginger hair shed pins
as fast as she stuck them in. She almost ran to
work, to find Miss Prescott, despite the fact that it
would be Christmas at the end of the week, in a
worse temper than usual. And as a consequence
Theodosia did nothing right. She dropped things,
spilt things, muddled up diet sheets and because of
that went late to her dinner.

It was cottage pie and Christmas pudding with
a blindingly yellow custard—and on her way back
she was to call in at Women's Medical and collect
two diet sheets for the two emergencies which had
been admitted. Because it was quicker, although
forbidden, she took the lift to the medical floor and
when it stopped peered out prudently before alight-
ing; one never knew, a ward sister could be passing.

There was no ward sister but the professor was
standing a few yards away, his arm around a
woman. They had their backs to her and they were
laughing and as Theodosia looked the woman

stretched up and kissed his cheek. She wasn't a young woman but she was good-looking and beautifully dressed.

Theodosia withdrew her head and prayed hard that they would go away. Which presently they did, his arm still around the woman's shoulders, and as she watched, craning her neck, Women's Medical ward door opened, Sister came out and the three of them stood talking and presently went into the ward.

Theodosia closed the lift door and was conveyed back to Miss Prescott's office.

'Well, let me have those diet sheets,' said that lady sharply.

'I didn't get them,' said Theodosia, quite beside herself, and, engulfed in feelings she hadn't known she possessed, she felt reckless. 'I went late to dinner and I should have had an hour instead of the forty minutes you left me. Someone else can fetch them. Why don't you go yourself, Miss Prescott?'

Miss Prescott went a dangerous plum colour. 'Theodosia, can I believe my ears? Do you realise to whom you speak? Go at once and get those diet sheets.'

Theodosia sat down at her desk. There were several letters to be typed, so she inserted paper into her machine and began to type. Miss Prescott hesitated. She longed to give the girl her notice on the spot but that was beyond her powers. Besides, with all the extra work Christmas entailed she had to have help in her office. There were others working in the department, of course, but Theodosia, lowly though her job was, got on with the work she was familiar with.

'I can only assume that you are not feeling yourself,' said Miss Prescott. 'I am prepared to overlook your rudeness but do not let it occur again.'

Theodosia wasn't listening; she typed the letters perfectly while a small corner of her brain went over and over her unexpected glimpse of the professor. With the woman he was going to marry, of course. He would have been showing her round the hospital, introducing her to the ward sisters and his colleagues, and then they would leave together in his car and go to his home...

As five o'clock struck she got up, tidied her desk, wished an astonished Miss Prescott good evening and went home. The bed-sitter was cold and gloomy; she switched on the lamps, turned on the fire, fed Gustavus and made herself a pot of tea. She was sad and unhappy but giving way to self-pity wasn't going to help. Besides, she had known that he was going to marry; he had said so. But she must avoid him at the hospital...

She cooked her supper and presently went to bed. She had been happy, allowing her happiness to take over from common sense. She had no doubt that sooner or later she would be happy again; it only needed a little determination.

So now, instead of hoping to meet him as she went round the hospital, she did her rounds with extreme caution. Which took longer than usual, of course, and earned Miss Prescott's annoyance. It was two days later, sharing a table with other late-comers from the wards and offices, that the talk became animated. It was a student nurse from Women's Medical who started it, describing in detail the companion Professor Bendinck had brought to see the ward. 'She was gorgeous, not very young, but then you wouldn't expect him to be keen on a young girl, would you? He's quite old…'

Theodosia was about to say that thirty-five wasn't old—a fact she had learned from one of her dancing partners at the ball—and even when he was wearing his specs he still looked in his prime. But she held her tongue and listened.

'She was wearing a cashmere coat and a little hat which must have cost the earth, and her boots…!' The nurse rolled expressive eyes. 'And they both looked so pleased with themselves. He called her "my dear Rosie", and smiled at her. You know, he doesn't smile much when he's on his rounds. He's always very polite, but sort of reserved, if you know what I mean. I suppose we'll be asked to fork out for a wedding present.'

A peevish voice from the other end of the table said, 'Those sort of people have everything; I bet he's loaded. I wonder where he lives?'

Theodosia wondered what they would say if she told them.

'Oh, well,' observed one of the ward clerks. 'I hope they'll be happy. He's nice, you know—opens doors for you and says good morning—and his patients love him.'

Someone noticed the time and they all got up and rushed back to their work.

Two more days and it would be Christmas Eve and she would be free. Her presents for the aunts were wrapped, her best dress brushed and ready on its hanger, her case already half packed with everything she would need for the weekend, Gustavus's favourite food in her shoulder bag. She should be able to catch a late-afternoon train, and if she missed it there was another one leaving a short while later. She would be at the aunts' well before bedtime.

She was almost at the hospital entrance on her way home that evening when she saw the professor. And he had seen her, for he said something to the house doctor he was talking to and began to walk towards her.

Help, thought Theodosia. She was so happy to see him that if he spoke to her she might lose all her good sense and fling herself at him.

And help there was. One of the path lab assistants, the one who had danced with her at the ball, was hurrying past her. She caught hold of his arm and brought him to a surprised halt.

'Say something,' hissed Theodosia. 'Look pleased to see me, as though you expected to meet me.'

'Whatever for? Of course I'm pleased to see you, but I've a train to catch…'

She was still holding his sleeve firmly. The professor was very close now, not hurrying, though; she could see him out of the corner of her eye. She smiled up at her surprised companion. She said very clearly, 'I'll meet you at eight o'clock; we could go to that Chinese place.' For good measure she kissed his cheek and, since the professor was now very close, wished him good evening. He returned her greeting in his usual pleasant manner and went out to his car.

'Whatever's come over you?' demanded the young man from the path lab. 'I mean, it's all very well, but I've no intention of taking you to a Chinese restaurant. For one thing my girl wouldn't stand for it and for another I'm a bit short of cash.' He goggled at her. 'And you kissed me!'

'Don't worry, it was an emergency. I was just pretending that we were keen on each other.'

He looked relieved. 'You mean it was a kind of joke?'

'That's right.' She looked over his shoulder and caught a glimpse of the Bentley turning out of the forecourt. 'Thanks for helping me out.'

'Glad I could help. A lot of nonsense, though.'

He hurried off and Theodosia walked back to her bed-sitter, then told Gustavus all about it. 'You see,' she explained, 'if he doesn't see me or speak to me, he'll forget all about me. I shan't forget him but that's neither here nor there. I daresay he'll have a holiday at Christmas and spend it with her. She's beautiful and elegant, you see, and they were laughing together...' Theodosia paused to give her nose a good blow. She wasn't going to cry about it. He would be home by now, sitting in his lovely drawing room, and Rosie would be sitting with him.

Which is exactly what he was doing, George and Max at his feet, his companion curled up on a sofa. They were both reading, he scanning his post, she leafing through a fashion magazine. Presently she closed it. 'You have no idea how delightful it is to have the whole day to myself. I've spent a small fortune shopping and I can get up late and eat food I haven't cooked myself. It's been heaven.'

The professor peered at her over his specs. 'And you're longing to see James and the children...'

'Yes, I am. It won't be too much for you having us all here? They'll give you no peace—it will be a houseful.' She added unexpectedly, 'There's something wrong, isn't there? You're usually so calm and contained, but it's as though something—or someone?—has stirred you up.'

'How perceptive of you, my dear. I am indeed stirred—by a pair of grey eyes and a head of ginger hair.'

'A girl. Is she pretty, young? One of your house doctors? A nurse?'

'A kind of girl Friday in the diet department. She's young—perhaps too young for me—perhaps not pretty but I think she is beautiful. And she is gentle and kind and a delight to be with.' He smiled. 'And her hair really is ginger; she wears it in a bunch on top of her head.'

His sister had sat up, the magazine on the floor. 'You'll marry her, Hugo?'

'Yes, if she will have me. She lives in a miserable attic room with a cat and is to spend Christmas with her only family—two great-aunts. I intend to drive her there and perhaps have a chance to talk…'

'But you'll be here for Christmas?'

'Of course. Perhaps I can persuade her to spend the last day of the holiday here.'

'I want to meet her. Pour me a drink, Hugo, and tell me all about her. How did you meet?'

The following day the professor did his ward rounds, took a morning clinic, saw his private patients in the afternoon and returned to the hospital just before five o'clock. He had made no attempt to look for Theodosia during the morning—he had been too busy—but now he went in search of her. He hadn't been unduly disturbed by the sight of her talking to the young fellow from the path lab. After all, she was on nodding terms with almost everyone in the hospital, excluding the very senior staff, of course. But he had heard her saying that she would meet him that evening; moreover, she had kissed him. He had to know if she had given her heart to the man; after all, he was young and good-looking and she had never shown anything other than friendliness with himself.

He reviewed the facts with a calm logic and made his way to the floor where Theodosia worked.

She came rushing through the door then slithered to a halt because, of course, he was standing in her way. Since he was a big man she had no way of edging round him.

'Oh, hello,' said Theodosia, and then tried again. 'Good evening, Professor.'

He bade her good evening, too, in a mild voice. 'You're looking forward to Christmas? I'll drive you to Finchingfield. The trains will be packed and running late. Could you manage seven o'clock?'

She had time to steady her breath; now she

clutched at the first thing that entered her head. On no account must she go with him. He was being kind again. Probably he had told his fiancée that he intended to drive her and Rosie had agreed that it would be a kindness to take the poor girl to these aunts of hers. She shrank from kindly pity.

'That's very kind of you,' said Theodosia, 'but I'm getting a lift—he's going that way, staying with friends only a few miles from Finchingfield.' She was well away now. 'I'm going to a party there—parties are such fun at Christmas, aren't they?' She added for good measure, 'He'll bring me back, too.'

She caught the professor's eye. 'He works in the path lab…'

If she had hoped to see disappointment on his face she was disappointed herself. He said pleasantly, 'Splendid. You're well organised, then.'

'Yes, I'm looking forward to it; such fun…' She was babbling now. 'I must go—someone waiting. I hope you have a very happy Christmas.'

She shot away, racing down the stairs. He made no attempt to follow her. That he was bitterly disappointed was inevitable but he was puzzled, too. Theodosia had been altogether too chatty and anxious to let him know what a splendid time she was going to have. He could have sworn that she had been making it up as she went along… On the other hand, she might have been feeling embarrassed; she had never been more than friendly but she could possibly be feeling awkward at not having mentioned the young man from the path lab.

He went back to his consulting rooms, saw his patients there and presently went home, where his manner was just as usual, asking after his sister's day, discussing the preparations for Christmas, for Rosie's husband and the two children would be arriving the next morning. And she, although she was longing to talk about Theodosia, said nothing, for it was plain that he had no intention of mentioning her.

And nor did he make any attempt to seek her out at the hospital during the following day. There was a good deal of merriment; the wards looked festive, the staff were cheerful—even those who would be on duty—and those who were able to left early. The professor, doing a late round, glanced at his watch. Theodosia would have left by now for it was almost six o'clock. He made his way to the path lab and found the young man who had been talking to Theodosia still there.

'Not gone yet?' he asked. 'You're not on duty over the weekend, are you?'

'No, sir, just finishing a job.'

'You live close by?' asked the professor idly.

'Clapham Common. I'm meeting my girlfriend and we'll go home together. I live at home but she's spending Christmas with us.'

'Ah, yes. There's nothing like a family gathering. You're planning to marry.'

'Well, as soon as Dorothy's sold her flat—her parents are dead. Once it's sold we shall put our savings together and find something around Clapham.'

'Well, I wish you the best of luck and a happy Christmas!'

The professor went on his unhurried way, leaving the young man with the impression that he wasn't such a bad old stick after all, despite his frequent requests for tests at a moment's notice.

The professor went back to his office; ten minutes' work would clear up the last odds and ends of his work for the moment. He had no idea why Theodosia had spun such a wildly imaginative set of fibs but he intended to find out. Even if she had left at five o'clock she would hardly have had the time to change and pack her bag and see to Gustavus.

He was actually at the door when he was bleeped...

Theodosia hurried home. Miss Prescott, true to form, had kept her busy until the very last minute, which meant that catching the early train was an impossibility. She would phone the aunts and say that she would be on the later train. Once in her room she fed an impatient Gustavus, changed into her second-best dress, brushed her coat, found her hat and, since she had time to spare, put on the kettle for a cup of tea. It would probably be chilly on the train and there would be a lot of waiting round for buses once she got to Braintree.

She was sipping her tea when someone knocked on the door, the knock followed by Mrs Towzer's voice. Theodosia asked her in, explaining at the same time that she was just about to leave for her train.

'Won't keep you then, love. Forgot to give you this letter—came this morning—in with my post. Don't suppose it's important. 'Ave a nice time at your auntys'. 'Aving a bit of a party this evening; must get meself poshed up. The 'ouse'll be empty, everyone off 'ome.' They exchanged mutual good wishes and Mrs Towzer puffed her way down the stairs.

The letter was in Great-Aunt Mary's spidery hand. Surely not a last-minute request to shop for some forgotten article? Unless it was something she could buy at the station there was no time for anything else.

Theodosia sat down, one eye on the clock, and opened the letter.

She read it and then read it again. Old family friends, an archdeacon and his wife, had returned to England from South America, wrote Aunt Mary. Their families were in Scotland and they did not care to make such a long journey over the holiday period.

'Your aunt Jessica and I have discussed this at some length and we have agreed that it is our duty to give these old friends the hospitality which our Christian upbringing expects of us. Christmas is a time for giving and charity,' went on Aunt Mary, and Theodosia could almost hear her vinegary voice saying it. As Theodosia knew, continued her aunt, the accommodation at the cottage was limited, and since she had no lack of friends in London who would be only too glad to have her as a guest over Christmas they knew she would understand. 'We shall, of course, miss you…'

Theodosia sat quite still for a while, letting her thoughts tumble around inside her head, trying to adjust to surprise and an overwhelming feeling that she wasn't wanted. Of course she had friends, but who, on Christmas Eve itself, would invite themselves as a guest into a family gathering?

Presently she got up, counted the money in her purse, got her shopping bag from behind the door, assured Gustavus that she would be back presently and left the house. There was no one around; Mrs Towzer was behind closed doors getting ready for the party. She walked quickly to a neighbouring street where there was a row of small shops. There was a supermarket at its end but she ignored it; there the shops would stay open for another hour

or so, catching the last-minute trade. Although she
had the money she had saved for her train ticket
she needed to spend it carefully.

Tea, sugar, butter and a carton of milk, cheese,
food for Gustavus and a bag of pasta which she
didn't really like but which was filling, baked
beans and a can of soup. She moved on to the
butcher, and since it was getting late and he
wouldn't be open again for three days he let her
have a turkey leg very cheap. She bought bacon,
too, and eggs, and then went next door to the
greengrocer for potatoes and some apples.

Lastly she went to the little corner shop at the
end of the row, where one side was given over to
the selling of bread, factory-baked in plastic bags,
and lurid iced cakes, the other side packed with
everything one would expect to find in a bazaar.

Theodosia bought a loaf and a miniature
Christmas pudding and then turned her attention to
the other side of the shop. She spent the last of her
money on a miniature Christmas tree, which was
plastic, with a few sprigs of holly, and very lastly
a small box of chocolates.

Thus burdened she went back to Mrs Towzer's.
The front door was open; there were guests for the
party milling about in the hall. She passed them
unnoticed and climbed the stairs.

'We are going to have a happy Christmas together,' she told Gustavus. 'You'll be glad, any-

way, for you'll be warm here, and I've bought you a present and you've bought me one, too.'

She unpacked everything, stowed the food away and then set the Christmas tree on the table. She had no baubles for it but at least it looked festive. So did the holly and the Christmas cards when she had arranged them around the room.

Until now she hadn't allowed her thoughts to wander but now her unhappiness took over and she wept into the can of soup she had opened for her supper. It wasn't that she minded so very much being on her own; it was knowing that the great-aunts had discarded her in the name of charity. But surely charity began at home? And she could have slept on the sofa...

She ate her soup, unpacked the weekend bag she had packed with such pleasure, and decided that she might as well go to bed. And for once, since there was no one else to dispute her claim, she would have a leisurely bath...

It was half past eight before the professor left the hospital and now that he was free to think his own thoughts he gave them his full attention. Obviously he had nothing to fear from the lad in the path lab. For reasons best known to herself, Theodosia had embarked on some rigmarole of her own devising—a ploy to warn him off? She might not love him but she liked him. A man of no conceit, he was aware of that. And there was something wrong somewhere.

He drove himself home, warned his sister and brother-in-law that he might be late back, sought out Meg in the kitchen and told her to get a room ready for a guest he might be bringing back with him. Then he got into his car, this time with George and Max on the back seat, and drove away.

His sister, at the door to see him off, turned to see Meg standing beside her.

'It'll be that nice young lady with the gingery hair,' said Meg comfortably. 'Dear knows where she is but I've no doubt he'll bring her back here.'

'Oh, I do hope so, Meg; she sounds just right for him. Should we wait for dinner any longer?'

'No, ma'am, I'll serve it now. If they're not back by midnight I'll leave something warm in the Aga.'

Once he had left the centre of the city behind, the streets were almost empty. The professor reached Bishop's Stortford in record time and turned off to Finchingfield.

There were lights shining from the windows of the great-aunt's house. He got out with a word to the dogs and thumped the knocker.

Mrs Trickey opened the door, still in her hat. She said, 'You're a bit late to come calling; I'm off home.'

The professor said in his calm way, 'I'd like to see Miss Theodosia.'

'So would I. She's not here, only that archdeacon and his wife wanting hot water and I don't know what—a fire in their bedroom, too. You'd best come in and speak to Miss Chapman.'

She opened the door into the drawing room. 'Here's a visitor for you, Miss Chapman, and I'll be off.'

Great-Aunt Jessica had risen from her chair. 'Professor, this is unexpected. May I introduce Archdeacon Worth and Mrs Worth, spending Christmas with us…?'

The professor's manners were beautiful even when he was holding back impatience. He said all the right things and then, 'I came to see Theodosia…'

It was Aunt Mary who answered him.

'These old family friends of ours are spending Christmas with us. Having just returned from South America, they had no plans for themselves. We were delighted to be able to offer them hospitality over the festive season.'

'Theodosia?' He sounded placid.

'I wrote to her,' said Aunt Mary. 'A young gel with friends of her own age—I knew that she would understand and have no difficulty in spending Christmas with one or other of them.'

'I see. May I ask when she knew of this arrangement?'

'She would have had a letter—let me see, when did I post it? She must have had it some time today, certainly. We shall, of course, be delighted to see her—when something can be arranged.'

He said pleasantly, 'Yes, we must certainly do that once we are married. May I wish you all a happy Christmas.' He wasn't smiling. 'I'll see myself out.'

He had driven fast to Finchingfield, and now he drove back to London even faster. He was filled with a cold rage that anyone would dare to treat his Theodosia with such unkindness! He would make it up to her for the rest of her life; she should have everything she had ever wanted—clothes, jewels, and holidays in the sun... He laughed suddenly, knowing in his heart that all she would want would be a home and children and love. And he could give her those, too.

The house was quiet as Theodosia climbed the stairs from the bathroom on the floor below. All five occupants of the other bed-sitters had gone home or to friends for Christmas. Only Mrs Towzer was in her flat, entertaining friends for the evening. She could hear faint sounds of merriment as she unlocked her door.

The room looked welcoming and cheerful; the

holly and the Christmas cards covered the almost bare walls and the Christmas tree, viewed from a distance, almost looked real. The cat food, wrapped in coloured paper, and the box of chocolates were arranged on each side of it and she had put the apples in a dish on the table.

'Quite festive,' said Theodosia to Gustavus, who was washing himself in front of the gas fire. 'Now I shall have a cup of cocoa and you shall have some milk, and we'll go to bed.'

She had the saucepan in her hand when there was a knock on the door. She remembered then that Mrs Towzer had invited her to her party if she wasn't going away for Christmas. She had refused, saying that she would be away, but Mrs Towzer must have seen her coming in with the shopping and come to renew her invitation.

How kind, thought Theodosia, and opened the door. The professor, closely followed by George and Max, walked in.

'Always enquire who it is before opening your door, Theodosia,' he observed. 'I might have been some thug in a Balaclava helmet.'

She stared up at his quiet face. And even like that, she thought, I would still love him... Since he had walked past her into the room there was nothing for it but to shut the door.

'I was just going to bed...' She watched as the

two dogs sat down side by side before the fire, taking no notice of Gustavus.

'All in good time.' He was leaning against the table, smiling at her.

'How did you know I was here?' She was pleased to hear that her voice sounded almost normal, although breathing was a bit difficult.

'I went to see your aunts.'

'My aunts, this evening? Surely not...?'

'This evening. I've just come from them. They are entertaining an archdeacon and his wife.'

'Yes, I know. But why?'

'Ah, that is something that I will explain.'

He glanced around him, at the tree and the holly and the cards and then at the tin of cocoa by the sink. Then he studied her silently. The shapeless woolly garment she was wearing did nothing to enhance her appearance but she looked, he considered, beautiful; her face was fresh from soap and water, her hair hanging around her shoulders in a tangled gingery mass.

He put his hands in his pockets and said briskly, 'Put a few things in a bag, dear girl, and get dressed.'

She goggled at him. 'Things in a bag? Why?'

'You are spending Christmas with me at home.'

'I'm not. I have no intention of going anywhere.' She remembered her manners. 'Thank you for asking me, but you know as well as I that it's not possible.'

'Why not—tell me?'

She said wildly, 'I saw you at the hospital. I wasn't spying or anything like that but I got out of the lift and saw you both standing there. You had your arm round her and she was laughing at you. How could you possibly suggest…?' She gave a great gulp. 'Oh, do go away,' she said, and then asked, 'Does she know you are here? Did she invite me, too?'

The professor managed not to smile. 'No, she doesn't but she expects you. And Meg has a room ready for you…'

'It is most kind of you,' began Theodosia, and put a hand on his arm. This was a mistake, for he took it, turned it over and kissed the palm.

'Oh, no,' said Theodosia in a small voice as he wrapped his great arms round her.

She wriggled, quite uselessly, and he said gently, 'Keep still, my darling; I'm going to kiss you.'

Which he did at some length and very thoroughly. 'I have been wanting to do that for a long time. I've been in love with you ever since we first met. I love you and there will be no reason for anything I do unless you are with me.'

Somewhere a nearby church clock struck eleven.

'Now get some clothes on, my love, and we will go home.'

Theodosia dragged herself back from heaven. 'I can't— Oh, Hugo, you know I can't.'

He kissed her gently. 'You gave me no chance to explain; indeed you flung that lad from the path lab in my face, did you not? My sister, Rosie, and her husband and children are spending Christmas with me. It was she you saw at the hospital and you allowed yourself to concoct a lot of nonsense.'

'Yes, well…' She smiled at him. 'Do you really want to marry me?'

'More than anything in the world.'

'You haven't asked me yet.'

He laughed then and caught her close again. 'Will you marry me, Theodosia?'

'Yes, yes, of course I will. I did not try to fall in love with you but I did.'

'Thank heaven for that. Now find a toothbrush and take off that woolly thing you are wearing and get dressed. You can have fifteen minutes. Gustavus and the dogs and I will doze together until you are ready.'

'I can't leave him.'

'Of course not; he is coming too.'

The professor settled in a chair and closed his eyes.

It was surprising how much one could do in a short time when one was happy and excited and without a care in the word. Theodosia was dressed, her overnight bag packed after a fashion, her hair swept into a topknot and the contents of her hand-bag checked in something like ten minutes. She said rather shyly, 'I'm ready…'

The professor got to his feet, put Gustavus into his basket, fastened the window, turned off the gas and went to look in the small fridge. He eyed the morsel of turkey and the Christmas pudding, but said merely, 'We'll turn everything off except the fridge. We can see to it in a few days; you won't be coming back here, of course.'

'But I've nowhere else—the aunts…'

'You will stay with me, and since you are an old-fashioned girl Meg shall chaperon you until I can get a special licence and we can be married.' He gave her a swift kiss. 'Now come along.'

He swept her downstairs and as they reached the hall Mrs Towzer came to see who it was.

'Going out, Miss Chapman? At this time of night?' She eyed the professor. 'You've been here before; you seemed a nice enough gent.' She stared at him severely. 'No 'anky-panky, I 'ope.'

The professor looked down his splendid nose at her. 'Madam, I am taking my future wife to spend Christmas at my home with my sister and her family. She will not be returning here, but I will call after Christmas and settle any outstanding expenses.'

'Oh, well, in that case... 'Appy Christmas to you both.' She looked at George and Max and Gustavus's whiskery face peering from his basket. 'And all them animals.'

Stuffed gently into the car, Theodosia said, 'You sounded just like a professor, you know—a bit stern.'

'That is another aspect of me which you will discover, dear heart, although I promise I will never be stern with you.' He turned to look to her as he started the car. 'Or our children.'

She smiled and wanted to cry, too, for a moment. From happiness, she supposed. 'What a wonderful day to be in love and be loved. I'm so happy.'

As they reached his house, the first strokes of midnight sounded from the church close by, followed by other church bells ringing in Christmas Day. The professor ushered his small party out of the car and into his house. The hall was quiet and dimly lit and George and Max padded silently to the foot of the stairs where they sat like statues. He closed the door behind him, set Gustavus in his basket on the table and swept Theodosia into his arms. 'This is what I have wanted to do—to wish you a happy Christmas in my own home—your home, too, my dearest.'

Theodosia, after being kissed in a most satisfactory manner, found her breath. 'It's true, it's all true? Dearest Hugo, Happy Christmas.' She stretched up and kissed him and then kissed him again for good measure.

**Modern Romance™**
...seduction and
passion guaranteed

**Tender Romance™**
...love affairs that
last a lifetime

**Sensual Romance™**
...sassy, sexy and
seductive

*Blaze.*
...sultry days and
steamy nights

**Medical Romance™**
...medical drama on
the pulse

**Historical Romance™**
...rich, vivid and
passionate

*29 new titles every month.*

*With all kinds of Romance for
every kind of mood...*

MILLS & BOON®

*Makes any time special™*

MAT4